Treasures of the Heart

Adventures of a Main Street Merchant

An Oakview Novel

By
Tanya Katnic

Annabooks, LLC.
Rancho Mirage

Treasures of the Heart
Copyright © 2021, Tanya Katnic. All Rights Reserved

Published in the United States by **Annabooks, LLC.**
69 Bordeaux, Rancho Mirage, CA 92271
www.annabooks.com

Manufactured in the United States of America

10 9 8 7 6 5 4 3 2 1

Library of Congress Cataloging-in-

ISBN-13: 978-0-9911887-9-6

Books by Tanya Katnic

Oakview Series:

Our Mother Away from Home

A Recipe for Love

Treasures of the Heart

Acknowledgements

For assistance, support, and advice, I give thanks to Roxanne Brandt, Noelle Reminiskey, Pamela Gibbons Toomey, Linda Matthews, Robert Nguyen, Annabooks, and my family.

Chapter One

With a steaming cup of chamomile tea in hand, and a blazing fire warming the great room of her Oakview home on this brisk January evening, Jackie Patterson sits back to reflect on the myriad events of the past six months.

A beauty at 40, she arranges her short blonde curly hair in a fashionable but no-nonsense style. A mere 5 feet 2 inches tall, she is stronger physically, mentally, and emotionally than she ever thought possible. It is a strength that was thrust upon her under the saddest of circumstances.

In August, her husband Patrick collapsed while running on a treadmill at the Oakview Gym. An English professor at Walker College, he was a healthy, active 40-year-old man who carved out time to run three 5K's each year. He served as a coach for his sons' teams: Riley (soccer) and Cooper (baseball).

But the autopsy at Oakview General Hospital staunchly belied those facts.

Patrick suffered from a silent myocardial infarction (SMI) or "silent heart attack," named as such because its symptoms lack the intensity of a classic heart attack.

Whereas a patient might suffer extreme chest pain, shortness of breath and dizziness in the course of a regular heart attack, SMI symptoms can feel mild and be brief and they often get confused for regular discomfort. Patients often ignore them.

The town of Oakview descended upon the Patterson family after Patrick's death in the form of hugs, casseroles, offers of babysitting, and an overflow crowd at Patrick's funeral at the Oakview Presbyterian Church.

Jackie had no desire or strength to write a eulogy or an obituary and depended on the Patterson family to complete those tasks.

Riley, 5, and Cooper, 7, were inconsolable and clung to their mother in their overwhelming grief.

Since the funeral, she had tried to restore some sense of normalcy for her children. Quite often, she reads to their classes. She volunteered as team mom for both of their teams as they began their new seasons and took them on a few small trips, including ones to San Diego and San Francisco.

The children especially loved riding the cable cars in San Francisco as they all explored the city, noshing on sourdough bread and savoring hot fudge sundaes at Ghirardelli.

Precious memories with her precious children.

As is routine every night, she looks in on them before turning in.

Riley's room is decked out in all things equine, as he loves horses. He has yet to experience riding atop one, but Jackie hopes to one day soon afford him this opportunity.

Cooper's room displays his love of sports, especially baseball. And his many medals and ribbons fill every inch of the bulletin board.

Jackie's home is a showplace. Since she was a stay-at-home mother up until two months ago, she could afford the time to research furniture and interior design ideas. Every lamp, every framed photo, and every throw pillow reflects her exquisite taste.

Because of her talents, her sister-in-law, Sabrina, the wife of Patrick's brother Parker, offered Jackie a part-time job at Main Street Treasures, a beautiful gift shop and boutique featuring clothing for all ages and sizes.

With Sabrina on maternity leave after giving birth to her daughter, Jackie started working a full-time schedule at Treasures.

The shop is located on Main Street, situated among other favorites of the town, including new offerings the Sandwich Station and Two Scoops of Happiness, an old-fashioned ice-cream parlor.

Jackie loves Treasures, so aptly named. A shopper can find a gift for any recipient, from toys to music boxes to books and beyond.

Whenever a new shipment arrives, she thinks of it as her personal treasure box. Not knowing what Sabrina ordered—even though there is a list somewhere--it is a joy to discover the contents of each box. One day it could be children's books, on another, stuffed animals and key chains with pictures of Oakview.

Today Jackie has four mystery boxes to open.

She was just unlocking Treasures at 9:00 when Archie Manfree from the Sandwich Station next door popped in with her daily soup. Jackie's best friend since high school, he left his job as a dancer in Las Vegas to return to his hometown and open his shop, utilizing the culinary skills he had honed over the years while cooking for friends.

Archie celebrated the grand opening of his train-themed shop just before Christmas. And he was so glad to be next door to his SBFF (straight BFF). His other BFF—his GBFF, or gay BFF—is Roger Meadows, a Realtor with Homeland Realtors.

"Girlfriend! How goes the day? Up for a little cheesy potato today?"

"Oh, Archie, that sounds wonderful! It's such a chilly day, and it looks like rain."

Archie was on the flamboyant side, with myriad aprons with bold colors and designs. Today he had on a sunflower-colored one with sunflower seeds strewn at the bottom. He handed over the soup and a small baguette.

"Gotta scoot! Have a catering gig for lunch. Fifty sub sandwiches! Can you imagine?"

"Archie, thanks so much! You have a great day!"

Jackie returned to the packages, just delivered by the UPS guy, Gus.

One of the boxes contained make-up sets, with lip gloss, lipstick, mascara and foundation. She'd have to check those out. But she had to be careful not to spend her whole salary at the store!

Another had baby bibs embroidered with "firsts": My first Mother's Day, My first Fourth of July, etc.

Another was filled with Oakview postcards which captured the town beautifully, in all of its oak-filled splendor.

The package that Jackie loved the most was one containing scented candles. After opening the package, she leaned in closely to indulge in the collective scent of vanilla blossom, sparkling citron, grapefruit, persimmon, and sea spray.

These days it is impossible to set aside time for a bath, with all of the activities that her children have going on, plus the responsibilities of the shop, but she filed a promise to herself to one day soon indulge in a bath, complete with scented candles.

Maybe when her kids stayed at their grandparents' house.

After lunch, Maisie Robinson from Oakview Cleaners, conveniently located next door to Treasures, popped by seeking a gift for her granddaughter.

There is a saying about relatives we are born with and the families we choose to belong to.

Last year, Maisie discovered a homeless man sleeping on her doorstep. She began to make an extra lunch each day and gave it to the man, whom she learned was named Bill Hamilton, as he set out on his impromptu adventures after leaving her store's cozy porch each morning.

One day, Bill disappeared and Maisie felt his absence strongly. He came back several weeks later, clean and dapper; she didn't recognize him. To Maisie's delight, Bill had eventually obtained a job at Oakview First Bank, where he met Veronica, whom he subsequently married.

And when their daughter Olivia Maisie was born, they declared Maisie an official grandmother. She was a first timer; she and her late husband were childless. Treasures served as a shopping "treasure trove" for Maisie, especially when it comes to Olivia.

"Maisie! So good to see you!" exclaimed Jackie. "How have you been?"

"Well, I am still here!" she declared. "At 72, I'm alive and kicking!"

Glancing around the store, Maisie alighted on the stuffed animals.

"Jackie, I need some gifts for my granddaughter, who is turning one next week. Do you have any ideas?"

"We have several gifts," said Jackie, "from stuffed animals to toys that can teach, some that light up, you name it. What does your granddaughter like?"

"Well, Olivia really likes anything that lights up. She is just mesmerized by them. How about this stuffed glow worm? She would really like that."

Maisie chose two dresses and the worm, and Jackie set her up with a gift bag for the purchases.

"Thank you, dear," said Maisie, going in for a warm hug. "I am so glad that you were here to help me."

"Any time, Maisie!"

Later that evening, Jackie sat down to dinner with Riley and Cooper. As is her custom, she inquired about their roses and thorns for that day, the good and not-so-good events that transpired at school and, afterward, at daycare.

"Well," said Riley as he dug into his chicken pot pie, "Piper Chapman got a bloody nose at recess and the nurse had to come *all* the way out to the playground. That would be a thorn. My rose was that Miss Williams chose me to read after lunch. She likes how I read!"

"You are a good reader, honey! One of the best I have ever heard. What about you, Cooper?"

"I got an A on my math test! That's my rose. Billy Martin kept bullying me. That's my thorn." Cooper's eyes lowered when he shared his thorn.

"What? What does Mrs. Johnson have to say about this? Has she witnessed that little creep bugging you?"

"I didn't say anything to her," Cooper confessed.

"Cooper, how often does this happen? And for how long has it been happening?" Jackie was incensed at this point.

"He has been bullying me since he started at the school right before Christmas. He makes fun of my glasses and calls me Four Eyes. And, because I am a good student, he calls me Nerdle the Turtle."

"Oh, Cooper, I am so sorry. You know what? People who bully make fun of what they don't have in their lives. Is this Billy a good student?"

"No, Mom, he sure isn't."

"Well, I am going to have to talk to Mrs. Johnson about this."

"You don't have to, Mom," Cooper said, a plaintive look across his freckled face.

"Oh, yes, I do."

On Monday, her day off, Jackie had an appointment with Bridget Johnson before classes began at Easton Academy.

The second-grade teacher was a tall, slender woman with short dark hair and, as she did at Back to School Night, appeared genial and welcoming.

"Nice to see you, Mrs. Patterson," she said, shaking Jackie's hand. "What may I do for you?"

"As I mentioned on the phone, Cooper has been harassed and bullied by Billy Martin continually since Billy's arrival at your school. I wanted to ask if you have overheard any of the mean comments he directed toward Cooper."

Jackie was anxious for a reply from the teacher, who seemed stunned.

"No, Mrs. Patterson, I haven't. I promise that I will keep my eyes and ears open in the future. Easton Academy has a zero-tolerance policy for bullying."

Jackie gave some more specifics on the bullying and stood to leave.

"Thank you, Mrs. Johnson," she said. "I appreciate the support."

With that, Jackie shifted her focus to the kindergarten room, where she was today's special reader.

She had heard via email from Miss Caroline Williams that the book du jour was *Corduroy*, written and illustrated by Don Freeman.

Corduroy is a teddy bear displayed on a toy shelf in a department store. He comes to life at night in the store, and eventually a girl named Lisa buys Corduroy with money from her piggy bank.

Jackie loves the time she spends reading to the students in kindergarten and second grade. Her major at Walker College was in elementary education, a profession she abandoned once she married Patrick and then had their babies.

She likes to have a chat after her reading session, something that Miss Williams wholeheartedly agreed to.

"So, kindergarteners, how many of you have ever been to Target?"

Twenty hands shot skyward.

"Well, what would you do if you spent the night in Target, and you could go anywhere in the store, like Corduroy did?"

Twenty hands again shot skyward. Jackie pointed to Trevor Jones.

"Well, Mrs. Patterson, I would go straight for the snack bar and eat everything in sight!"

Everyone laughed and started to chatter.

Jackie pointed to Piper Chapman, she of the bloody nose last week.

"Mrs. Patterson, I would go to the furniture department and sleep in one of those huge beds they have!"

"That is a really practical idea, Piper!" exclaimed Jackie.

After she had called on everyone except Riley, she asked her son what his desire was.

"I wouldn't want to be alone in Target all night by myself, so I would invite you and Cooper to join me, where we would play with all of the games all night long!"

"Sounds like fun!" Jackie loved this sensitive, loving child more than life itself.

Since she had several hours to herself before fetching her children at the end of school, Jackie decided to grab lunch at the Sandwich Station.

She loved coming here, not because her friend and confidant was the proprietor, but because the environment was just priceless.

Inspired by his family's ties to the railroad, most recently Amtrak, Archie had displayed posters of railroad cars and even had set up a small group of four cars that traversed the restaurant on a set of rails suspended from the ceiling.

The effect was stunning, and it drew Oakviewites in droves, especially when Archie opened his doors in December.

"Honey! What brings you by? Dining solo?" Archie came around the corner to hug Jackie. Today his apron was black, and the message was in white letters: "I cook as good as I look."

Jackie just smiled.

"You got it, Archie. I read in Riley's class this morning after I had a long talk with Cooper's teacher. It seems that he has been bullied by some jerk in his class."

"Well, well! I wrote the book on how to respond to bullies, my dear. Just look at me, and imagine a mini-me of years gone by. I know that I pivoted immensely in high school to become oh-so-popular, but things were different before you knew me."

He struck a pose, his head raised and his red hair perfectly coiffed.

"This was the victim of many bullies."

He continued as he showed Jackie to her booth, "Bring young Cooper over sometime. We will have a little tete-a-tete, man to man. Or, me to him!" He chuckled.

"Thanks, Archie. You are a real friend. I would love to have the Caesar salad and an iced tea, if you want to tell my server."

"I will personally inform the chef," said Archie, winking upon his exit as he sashayed across the restaurant.

When Jackie and the children arrived home that afternoon, there were several cars in the cul-de-sac where they lived. People seemed to be coming in and out of the Walters house next door. One of them was the Oakview Chief of Police, Bryan Stanley.

Jackie was curious as to the meaning of the throng.

"Hi Bryan," she addressed the chief. "What the heck is happening at the Walters'?"

"Well, as you know, Mikey has a paper route before school. This morning around 7:00, he was hit by a drunken driver between here and the town square. Who is drunk at 7:00 in the morning?"

"That is just awful, Bryan! How is Mikey?"

Jackie was really concerned for her neighbor, who had become like a third child to her. His mother, Elisabeth Walters, died of breast cancer three years ago, and his father Jason had morphed into the most unpleasant neighbor anyone could ever have.

"His arm is broken, but he was able to recall all of the events of this morning. Poor guy," said Chief Stanley.

"Do you think we might be able to visit him this evening?" Jackie thought that the kids might want to make some homemade cards to bring to Mikey.

"That is totally up to you-know-who," Bryan said, nodding in the direction of the house next door. "Don't want to use any bad language around your kids," he said, and Jackie nodded in agreement.

Everyone knew that Jason Walters was the meanie on the block, the curmudgeon, the sourpuss. He adopted that persona when his wife fell ill, and it stuck with him. It was as if he were mad at the whole world.

An accountant who works from home, Jason is constantly shooing people off his property, even if they have a purpose to be there. Girl Scouts, the gas company representative, you name it. He shoos them like they are chickens.

Jason really is a nice-looking man in his 40's: blond hair and blue eyes, and a great physique thanks to his workout sessions at Oakview Gym during his lunch break when his son is at school.

However, his nastiness detracts from his physical attributes, and he is unaware that he is doing a great disservice to himself with his terrible demeanor.

But Mikey, a sophomore at Bennington High School, is a great kid despite his father. He loves Riley and Cooper and often babysits for them. They adore him.

After saying goodbye to Bryan and letting the kids into the house, Jackie ventured next door and steeled herself to face the meanie.

"Hello, Mr. Walters," Jackie greeted him as he answered the door. She never, ever called him Jason. She wouldn't give him the satisfaction.

"The kids and I are really concerned about Mikey and wondered when we could pay him a visit."

"Well, he isn't up to visitors," barked Jason. "Come back another day."

With that, he quickly slammed the door in Jackie's face.

"Cretin! Monster! Jerk!" Jackie whispered her personal nicknames for Jason under her breath as she walked home, as if in a twisted mantra.

No way would she voice such appellations aloud in front of her children.

Dinner was followed by homework and television, and bedtime commenced after baths and story time.

Jackie liked to inject some fun into the kids' weekends, and she inquired about their desires for the upcoming one during reading breaks.

"I want to go to Two Scoops of Happiness," announced Cooper. "I'll get a scoop of vanilla and a scoop of chocolate chip."

"Wow, that sounds delicious!" said Jackie. "What would you like to do, Riley?"

"I want to go to the library and check out some books," he said. Riley was not only a great reader in the spoken sense, but he simply devoured books.

"Okay, after Riley's soccer game on Saturday, we will go to Two Scoops of Happiness. And on Sunday after lunch we will go to the library and find some books for both of you."

Cooper wasn't too keen on reading, but he agreed to the plan.

Anything to bring normalcy to their lives, thought Jackie.

Main Street Treasures was only open until 12:00 on Saturday, and Jackie had Sundays and Mondays off, so she was able to make afternoon games on Saturdays. She had a back-up "parent" in Archie, who had taken the kids to a few early Saturday games. He loves her kids, who call him Uncle Archie.

Just as she was about to close up shop at 11:55, her mother-in-law, Patsy Castleberry, came through the door.

"Patsy! What a wonderful surprise!" Jackie came around the counter to hug Patsy, who was like a mirror image of her: Both were just over five feet tall and blonde, but Patsy had straight hair and Jackie had a mop of curls.

Patsy was the best mother-in-law in the world, according to Jackie, Sabrina, and Cassie, Pete's wife.

When Jackie was falling apart in the wake of Patrick's death, Patsy was there to catch her. A widow, retired nurse and nursing professor at Walker College, Patsy was her rock, and the support that she got from Patsy and her second husband James was immeasurable.

The biggest contribution that the Castleberrys make is paying tuition for Cooper and Riley at Easton Academy.

Sometimes Jackie feels as if the Pattersons, Castleberrys, Archie and her children are her only family, with her parents' recent move to Florida and her estrangement from her sister Rachel, who left Oakview ten years ago and never returned.

Rachel was madly in love with Patrick, though they were in a platonic relationship. When Jackie returned home from the University of Southern California one summer, she and Patrick connected in a non-platonic way and Rachel fled. She didn't even attend Patrick's funeral. And she had no idea that he and Jackie had two children.

So many times, Jackie went to pick up the phone and call Rachel who, according to Jackie, had "laughing hazel eyes" when she was happy. But she didn't even know Rachel's present phone number. Her phone number from ten years ago didn't connect.

Jackie missed Rachel tremendously and had no idea where her sister was.

"I know that you are just closing up, but I wanted to quickly drop by while I was in town visiting the baby girls," said Patsy.

"Sabrina looks so great, it's amazing. And Chris and Drew are proud big brothers to little Amelia. And Cassie's little Rosalie is so precious! I knew that I would get some granddaughters one day!"

Patsy had four grandsons before the girls came along.

She continued, "You are never going to guess what happened! As you know, James and I are avid *Wheel of Fortune* viewers, and we auditioned to be on their Valentine's Day special—newlyweds only could apply."

"They chose us to be on the show! Can you imagine when a 60-something (she pointed to herself) and a 70-something show up as newlyweds! The place will go crazy!" Patsy predicted.

The Castleberrys, both widowed, were introduced by Patsy's daughter-in-law Cassie when Patsy was a guest speaker in Cassie's sophomore health class, and James came to the school to have lunch with the principal.

"Patsy! That is so great! When will the episode air?" asked Jackie.

"James and I will be hosting a watch party on Valentine's Day, which is a Friday. That is the air date. I hope that you, the kids, and Archie can come. I would love for you all to spend the night, as you have the longest commute."

Oakview was 45 minutes away from James and Patsy's house in Marina Shores.

"We will all be there!"

She added, "Hey, Patsy! Make sure you pop in next door and see Archie. He loves his Mama P!"

After Patsy left, Jackie thought how blessed Patsy and James were to find each other so late in life.

Maybe there's hope for me, she thought, and stopped herself abruptly.

Why am I thinking of dating again? That sure came out of nowhere. She quickly filed that thought away for another day.

On Tuesday, the Chamber of Commerce met at 8:00 in the *Oakview Register* building.

Laney, the managing editor of the paper, had just celebrated eight months of sobriety, and the transformation was not only internal but external.

She seemed to shine from within and no longer dressed in risqué clothing. Today she had on a beautiful blue pant suit which accented her sparkling blue eyes.

Harley Keffer, the boss of Oakview First Bank, was in the middle of his tenure as president of the Chamber.

"Welcome, everyone! So good to see you all here. Thank you, Laney, for graciously hosting our meeting."

He glanced at the goody table, resplendent with scones, jelly donuts and chocolate croissants.

"I take it those are from Sandy's Dandies," he prognosticated. "Lucky us!"

Sandy Thomas just beamed.

"Okay," said Harley, "let's take a glance at the agenda."

The group discussed the upcoming Sweetheart Dance, which will be held in the gym at Bennington High School on February 8 and will be open to all citizens of Oakview. Proceeds from the sale of tickets will go towards the Oakview Senior Center.

Chief Stanley noted that there was a break-in at the Speedy Gas in the early hours of Monday. The proprietor, Justin Bell, came in to the gas station when he received an alert on his watch, only to find the place ransacked. Under $100 was taken from the register.

The chief said that this was a cautionary tale for everyone.

Archie chimed in next.

"Chief, I understand that everyone here has a special panic button with a signal that goes straight to the police station upon hitting it. How can I get one of those? I just don't feel as protected as everyone else is. I know I'm the new kid on the block, but I would really like one of those gizmos."

Today Archie's apron was emblazoned with trains and the Sandwich Station logo.

"I would like one too," said Brenda Finch of Two Scoops of Happiness.

"I promise to install one in each of your stores by the end of the week," the chief said. "We all have to be at the ready in case there's an emergency."

Just before 9:00, Harley made his final announcement.

"Before I conclude this meeting, I want to tell you that something very exciting is on the horizon for Oakview and its citizens, but I can't tell you about it yet," he said.

"Come on, Harley! You can't just dangle a carrot in front of all of us, then zip your lip," declared Maisie as she stood and placed her hands on her frail hips after making a zipping move over her lips.

"Trust me. It will be worth it," Harley portended, a sly smile on his secretive lips.

Chapter Two

January was about to close its books with its characteristically chilly persona on display, as the days grew shorter and night seemed to creep in earlier every day.

Riley made the all-star soccer team, which meant extra games in the offing. Luckily, the games were in the evenings.

Little League seemed to have an extra-long season, and continued during the winter months. Cooper was becoming a shining star as a pitcher, and Coach John was pleased with his performance.

While Jackie and Cooper were watching one of Riley's games, she brought up the subject of bullying.

"Honey, has Billy Martin been bugging you still? Has Mrs. Johnson said anything to you?'

"Mrs. Johnson overheard Billy calling me Nerdle the Turtle and she talked to him. He hasn't said anything to me since."

He added, "She ended class early yesterday to give us a talk on bullying and name calling. She said that the school has a zero topperance for bullying, whatever that means."

Jackie tried not to laugh.

"It means that the school—and the principal, vice principals, teachers and staff—will not allow bullying to happen at Easton Academy. It is called zero tolerance. Tolerance means to put up with something," she said, making a teaching experience out of the discussion.

"That makes me feel better," said Cooper, a huge weight off his frail seven-year-old shoulders.

A few days later, Jackie appeared at the Walters' doorstep once again, this time with her children in tow, who clutched homemade get-well cards.

Again, Jason answered the door, a scowl across his handsome face.

"Yes?" he blurted out, and glanced at his watch as if the Pattersons were infiltrating his precious time.

"Mr. Walters, my children made cards for Mikey. May we come inside for a visit with him?"

Jackie bit the bullet and tried the saccharin approach, thinking of the adage about catching more flies with honey than vinegar.

"I guess," he said. "But you have five minutes before I call him to dinner. And, children, be very gentle around him because of his cast. Mikey is in the den."

As her kids flew into the house in the direction of the den, Jackie could only shrug her shoulders at Jason. But secretly she was glad that they barreled by him.

It seemed as if the three children hadn't seen each other in months, instead of just over a week.

They were all talking at once.

"Did the drunk driver get hurt?" asked Cooper.

"Are you in pain?" Riley was concerned for his friend.

"Tell me about your sports," Mikey requested.

Jackie came into the den to restore some order and to gently hug the patient.

"Mikey, we have been so worried about you! How are you feeling?" she asked.

"Well, I am a bit sore still. I have to have this cast on for three more weeks, and I can't do my paper route until then. That's the real bummer. I am out four weeks' pay because of a drunken driver."

He continued, "To answer your question, Squirt (his name for Cooper), the driver hit me and then hit a tree. Her car was totaled. She was taken away in an ambulance, just like me."

"Oh!" Riley yelped. "What is it like inside an ambulance?"

"Even though I was in so much pain, it was really exciting to be going through the streets of Oakview at like 100 miles an hour! My dad was allowed to be in the ambulance with me. They took me to Oakview General Hospital."

Speak of the devil, or the cretin, as Jackie might say. Precisely five minutes since their arrival at the Walters', Jason came into the den and stopped the chatter, announcing that it was dinner time.

Cooper and Riley gave Mikey their cards and everyone hugged carefully.

"We will see you soon!" exclaimed Jackie, who offered the final hug.

She hoped that next time their visit wouldn't be measured by a kitchen timer.

Jackie was in the middle of doing inventory when Archie popped in to make an announcement and to offer some beef barley soup and a roast beef sandwich.

Today his apron bore hearts and flowers, a nod to Valentine's Day, which was fast approaching.

"Well, I have had this idea percolating since I opened next door. I would like to do some kind of promotion and the winner will get coupons for a free month of sandwiches. The people who come in second and third will get a week's worth of sandwiches," Archie announced.

"That's great, Archie! What kind of promotion do you have in mind?" Jackie was curious.

"I was thinking that I would invent a new sandwich, and those who enter the contest will offer names for it. We will have a panel of judges and have KFUNN, the *Register,* and Mayor Max here for the unveiling of the name."

He sighed deeply. "Any excuse to have Mayor Max here!"

"Pipe down! He's a married man!" exclaimed Jackie. "Though I have to admit, he's a cutie!"

She shifted her focus.

"I really like your idea, Archie. It will be a great promotion for your store. Can I be one of the judges?"

"Absolutely, girlfriend! I am going to ask a bunch of merchants to be judges. They will do the judging ahead of time and make the announcement the day of the unveiling. Let me ask Maisie, Sandy, and Mario from the Pizza Project. Oh, and maybe his wife, Debra, from the Pizza Project #2. Heck, I'll invite the entire Chamber of Commerce!"

He gave two claps of his hands, then raised his arms skyward.

"This is beyond fabulous!" he declared.

On her next day off, Jackie was slated to read in Cooper's second-grade class. In conference with Mrs. Johnson, she was ready to read *Stand Tall, Molly Lou Melon* by Patty Lovell.

Molly Lou is a unique little girl whose grandmother has taught her to always walk proudly and smile brightly. So when the class bully, Ronald Durkin, begins to harass her, she wins him over with her confidence.

Jackie didn't need to know which student was Billy Martin. His eyes were filled with tears by the end of her reading.

Instead of addressing the issue of bullying, she took another tack in her chat time.

"Students, one of the biggest lessons that we get from this book is that we all have flaws. What does that mean?"

"That means that there are things within us that aren't perfect," declared Claire Nesbit, looking very pleased with her answer.

"That is a wonderful answer, Claire! Nobody is perfect, so we need to accept that fact and embrace our flaws. They make us who we are," said Jackie, glancing at Billy.

After she bade the second graders goodbye, Jackie noticed that Billy went up to Cooper and hugged him. Then, they set off together to recess.

Jackie just smiled as she watched the boys fly out the door and was glad that she was part of this small victory.

The Sweetheart Dance brought out many citizens of Oakview to the gym at Bennington, which was resplendent in red hearts and streamers, courtesy of the school's Associated Student Body.

Jackie, her kids, and Archie came dressed in the requisite red, and enjoyed the camaraderie of their friends and neighbors. Also in attendance was Archie's friend Roger, the Realtor.

Chief Stanley, dressed in civilian clothes, looked dapper as he approached Jackie and asked her to dance.

"It's nice to just be friends with you," said Jackie when the music stopped.

She was alluding to their very brief attempt at dating.

"Yes, it is nice," echoed Bryan, who secretly wished that they hadn't given up the dating scene. He found Jackie very attractive.

Jackie was checking on her kids—who were in the kids' zone—when she spotted Jason and Mikey Walters, Mikey minus the cast.

"Your cast is off! How wonderful!" Jackie exclaimed. "Are you returning to your paper route?"

"Yes, on Monday bright and early! Now I can make a living again!" boasted Mikey.

Jackie chuckled, and the chuckling stopped when she locked eyes with Jason, who had his permanent scowl plastered across his bitter face.

"Mikey, the kids are in the kids' zone, where there are games and cards. You can even make a homemade Valentine," Jackie suggested.

"Okay! Dad, I'll be over there," Mikey said as he dashed towards the Patterson children.

In an awkward turn of events, Jackie and Jason were standing so close that she could smell his woodsy aftershave.

To bolt or to stay? That was the question she asked herself.

"Would you like to dance?" he asked, offering his hand to her as the DJ played "Wonderful Tonight" by Eric Clapton.

Jackie didn't speak as she took his hand and they glided to the dance floor.

It seemed that all of Oakview was staring at them, completely perplexed that Jason chose to dance with the lady next door. This seemed way out of his comfort zone.

Jackie tried to think of the words to her negative mantra about Jason, but she could only think pleasant thoughts about this handsome man who was holding her gently and smelling like a hunk in an aftershave commercial.

She was afraid that the sparks that they were igniting were visible to the audience, who were pointing and chatting, pointing and chatting.

When the music ended, he said "Thank you" and left the dance floor.

Sabrina Patterson, on a date with her husband Parker, scooted over to Jackie, who was completely stunned.

"So, the boy next door can dance!" Sabrina said, throwing her arms around her sister-in-law.

"That was completely out of nowhere!" admitted Jackie. "I think for maybe three minutes he forgot to scowl!"

Thoughts of Jason subsided as the two caught up, mostly about Main Street Treasures.

But later that night, thoughts of Jason haunted Jackie's dreams and made her feel like a desirable woman for the first time in a long while.

On Valentine's Day, the entire Patterson gang filed into Patsy and James's huge home in Marina Shores, which James had remodeled to include 8 bedrooms, 6 bathrooms, and an extra-large living room.

All told, there were 16 adults and 19 children, who dined on Italian food created by Patsy, the ultimate party planner. She actually worked with the activities director at Marina Shores High School during the previous school year, planning dances and other activities. James was the principal for that one year.

Now, both she and her husband were retired.

"Grandma, can I listen to your heartbeat?" asked Riley, as she brought Patsy her ever-present black bag filled with medical equipment.

"Sure, honey. Let me set you up."

With that, Patsy put the ear pieces of the stethoscope in Riley's tiny ears and Riley beamed with delight and listened to his grandmother's heart.

"I think this one wants to work in the medical field," said Patsy as Jackie sat next to her on the couch. "He loves my bag of tricks!"

"He sure does," said Jackie. "I am thinking of getting him a kid's version for his birthday next month."

"Let me do it!" said Patsy. "I know just where to go."

James summoned everyone to take a seat.

Wheel of Fortune was about to begin. The viewers were all talking at once, and they finally all settled down when the opening music began.

Pat Sajak welcomed the four newlywed couples and was taken aback when he saw James and Patsy among them.

"Are you sure you're newlyweds?" he joked.

"We are, Pat," said James. "We have been married for two and a half years. I have my daughter-in-law, Cassie, to thank, as she introduced us."

The room erupted when Patsy and James won the game and were poised to go to the bonus round.

Of course, the couple was sworn to secrecy about the game, which was taped a month ago. A month is a long time to keep silent!

After spinning the prize wheel, they stepped up to their marks and Pat announced that R, S, T, L, N and E were freebies. Patsy and James were to choose three more consonants and one more vowel.

They chose W, C, F and I.

With the letters filled in, the board read: IN WE_ _E_ _LISS.

James and Patsy started jumping up and down on the television screen, and the clan was now on its feet, doing the same.

"We'd like to solve the puzzle, Pat," blurted Patsy, breathlessly.

She and James together shouted out "IN WEDDED BLISS!" and hugged tightly.

"Way to go, you newlyweds! Now, let's see what your prize is," said Pat.

He opened the folder; it read $100,000!

Everyone went berserk. Sabrina's baby started to cry and the grandchildren jumped all over the winners. High fives and hugs abounded.

James addressed the crowd when the show was over.

"As you know, Patsy and I have been sworn to secrecy for the last month, and that gave us time to consider how to spend our money. Patsy, will you please do the honors?"

With that, she distributed tickets to Maui for the entire family, including Archie.

More eruption from the crowd.

"We will all travel together as a family this summer. As you all know, Maui is your mother's favorite place in the world and where we got married.

The last time many of you were on the island was to scatter your father's ashes into the ocean."

He nodded to Patsy's boys.

"Now we will go to celebrate our victory. We wanted all of you with us."

Later that evening, Patsy came into the kitchen and opened the refrigerator to the snacking possibilities. She was surprised when Archie joined her.

"Can't sleep, honey?" she inquired.

Archie nodded, and made a confession.

"Sleep has been eluding me of late. I just got some medical news that I was going to share with you at a later date. I didn't want to spoil this wonderful celebration."

Tears began to fall as he quickly wiped them away.

"What is it, honey?"

Patsy was pouring milk into cereal and stopped mid-pour.

"Mama P, I have prostate cancer," Archie admitted. "I have had a second opinion and have undergone lots of tests."

"Oh, I am so sorry, Archie," said Patsy as she threw her arms around him. "How are you feeling?"

"Scared, vulnerable, terrified of the future," said Archie, clinging to Patsy's arms.

"And you are aware of the possible side effects of prostate cancer surgery?" Patsy inquired.

"Yes, impotence and incontinence," said Archie as he winced, imagining the worst. "I have been schooled in the side effects."

She just had to ask.

"Have you told Jackie?"

"Not yet. I was going to tell her soon, as the surgery is in 20 days." Archie's pained expression said it all.

"Well, Archie, I will be there for you, for surgery and beyond. I will spend some time with Jackie and the kids, and will help you post-surgery," promised Patsy.

"Oh, Mama P! Thank you!!! I love you so much!"

With that, there was nonstop hugging, and tears from both of them fell freely.

"I love you, too, honey," whispered Patsy.

Chapter Three

Jackie was enjoying the quiet of Main Street Treasures early one morning as she dusted the shelves and took in the magical pieces on display. She stopped to inspect a jewelry box that seemed to have a piece of paper peeking out of its bottom drawer.

She opened the drawer to find a collection of letters that were yellowed and written in a beautiful hand. There were no envelopes.

Almost feeling as if she were violating someone's privacy, Jackie chose the top letter to find a very romantic message:

Dearest Margaret,

I miss you terribly. Time is moving slowly here in Costa Rica and I am counting the days until I am dismissed from the Peace Corps. As of today, I have 39 days left until I can be in your arms again.

I almost feel guilty. I entered the Corps to help mankind, but I had no idea that I would meet

*you just weeks before heading here. I know
that I have a job to do, but I so wish I were
with you instead.*

Until I am free, I remain yours truly.

Robby

Just then, Cassie Patterson, her other sister-in-law, entered the store, her tiny one-month-old, Rosalie, in tow. She passed the baby to Jackie after they hugged.

"Oh, Cassie! Rosalie is just beautiful!" Jackie beamed. "How are you all doing?"

"We are all doing great!" gushed Cassie. "Sleep-deprived, but great!"

Cassie continued, "It's Pete's birthday next week, and I wanted to see if you have any Hawaiian shirts. He could use some for the big vacation!"

Cassie browsed the brightly colored collection of shirts while Jackie relished the sweet scent of Rosalie. She smelled of baby powder and baby essence, and Jackie was in heaven.

"This brings me back," said Jackie. "I just can't resist babies and their precious scent."

"Rosalie is a good baby so far. We are just learning by doing. I know that it will get easier," said Cassie.

When Cassie left, Jackie flew to her cell phone and dialed Sabrina's number. She couldn't wait to tell her about the discovery of the love letters.

Jackie was overjoyed when Sabrina picked up, and explained her treasure find.

"Gosh, that must have been one of the donations or consignment items we received over the past month or so. I sincerely don't know the origin. Well, I guess those letters are challenging you to find the recipient," said Sabrina.

"Yes, I guess that is my quest!" said Jackie, up for the challenge.

She was about to peruse another letter when Archie walked in, lentil soup and a tuna melt sandwich in hand.

Today, his apron was pink—it is his usual one for October, Breast Cancer Awareness Month. It read "Never give up. Never give in."

He wore it for a reason.

"Archie! Thanks so much! How are you doing?" asked Jackie as Archie handed over her lunch. He was looking dejected and defeated.

"Have a seat, girlfriend. I have something to tell you, and it's full of bad juju."

Archie's usually jovial demeanor vanished as he explained what was in store for him in 19 short days.

Jackie sobbed. Before her was her BFF, her partner in crime at Bennington High School, especially in the drama department when they were in plays and musicals together.

Like Patsy, Archie was part of her support system and had played an integral part in her life.

"Oh, Archie, I am so, so sorry!" Upon hearing the sad news, Jackie jumped up and hugged Archie, wanting to magically pass her strength along to him.

"Everything will be okay, BFF. Patsy is going to come help me. She's going to ask you if she can stay at your house for a while," said Archie.

"That's wonderful!" exclaimed Jackie. "You and I are so fortunate to have Patsy in our lives."

"Boy, are we," agreed Archie. A strong sense of comfort punctuated his words.

"Okay, kids, time to leave for school," Jackie advised as she was packing the kids' lunches on a Friday morning.

Just as they were leaving the house, Jason Walters was coming up their walkway.

Flashing back to the Valentine Dance, Jackie was momentarily caught off guard and lost in thought, remembering their mesmerizing dance.

But not for long.

"Mrs. Patterson, it seems as if the stupid mail carrier gave me all of your mail yesterday," snarled Jason as he shot a stack of mail Jackie's way.

"Mr. Walters, the mail carrier is not stupid. He is young and just starting out in his career with the post office," Jackie retorted, with a snarl to match Jason's.

"Whatever," he snapped, pivoted, and returned to his house.

Cretin. Monster. Jerk. It all came back to her.

Voting for the new sandwich's name was now closed online and in the Sandwich Station. Archie got some interesting names for his new sandwich.

The Chamber of Commerce commenced at Archie's restaurant for their monthly meeting. Archie had prepared sandwiches for everyone, who seemed to be enjoying them, even though it was 8:00 in the morning.

After Harley opened the meeting, he gave the floor to Archie.

"Good morning, friends!" he beamed, as he began to distribute sandwiches and bottles of water.

"Before you we have the newest sandwich at the Sandwich Station. Choo-choo!" Archie just couldn't stop himself, and pulled an imaginary train whistle. Today he donned the restaurant's signature apron.

"The sandwich consists of applewood smoked bacon, brie cheese, and turkey on grilled sourdough bread."

He felt like a giddy contestant on one of those cooking shows on the Food Network who, proffering their dish, say something like, "Today I have for you a yogurt-marinated grilled chicken shawarma with grilled onions and tomatoes, accompanied by pita bread and toum, a Lebanese garlic sauce."

Archie continued, "I have the list of entries printed out for you. Let's vote after you peruse them and enjoy your sandwiches."

There was much chatting among the Chamber folks, but eventually they settled on a title for the sandwich, which would be revealed at the naming ceremony.

Jackie was opening Main Street Treasures later that morning when Maisie paid a visit.

"What did you think of that sandwich, Jackie?" Maisie asked, a giant frown on her wrinkled face. "I have never heard of brie cheese before! Give me a slice of good old American cheese and I am happy!"

Jackie laughed and said, "Well, Maisie, brie is a soft, spreadable cheese. It's a trendy cheese that sometimes comes cooked with a layer of puff pastry surrounding it. That is just delicious!"

"Still, I'll stick with the American," said Maisie, waving a hand as she exited Treasures.

With no customers in sight, Jackie dipped into the treasure box of letters to find one filled with hope.

My dear Margaret,

I think of you incessantly and wonder what you are doing. Are you off with your friends to a matinee, or maybe doing homework or contemplating your graduation in June?

My days are numbered here in Costa Rica: 25 to go.

25 days until I get to see you, my beloved. 25 days until I can look into your beautiful brown eyes and perceive the soul of my one and only.

All my love,
Robby

She dipped into the box again to find a lighthearted letter.

>*My love, my Margaret,*
>
>*One of the perks of being in a Spanish-speaking country is learning the language!*
>
>*In high school, I studied French, but I have learned that some Spanish and French words are similar.*
>
>*Here are just a few examples of things I've picked up:*
>
>*I have learned to say "Hola, mi amigo." It means "Hello, my friend."*
>
>*And "Plantemos algunas verduras." It means "Let's plant some vegetables."*
>
>*And "Buen trabajo," which means "Good job."*
>
>*And my favorite, "Te quiero," which means "I love you."*
>
>*Te quiero, dear Margaret*
>*Robby*

Jackie marveled at the love that was emanating from Robby's heart and soul. She thought that Margaret was one lucky lady.

Gus, the UPS guy, appeared at her door, boxes in hand. He was a muscle-bound young man whom

Archie doted on. Too bad Gus didn't play on Archie's team.

"Hey, Jackie! I have these for you today," said Gus, who filled out his brown uniform quite nicely.

"Thanks, Gus! Have a good day!"

Jackie opened up the box of treasures to find Oakview T-shirts in men's sizes and women's sunglasses. She was a bit disappointed that the items weren't treasure-like.

The next Saturday Jackie closed up the shop early so that she would be at the Sandwich Station for the naming ceremony.

Oakviewites filled the restaurant and the crowd spilled out onto the sidewalks of Main Street.

There was much chatting going on as the town stood in anticipation of the announcement of the winners.

A photographer from the *Oakview Register* was on hand, as was DJ PJ Panda from KFUNN radio.

Mayor Max, as usual, gave a little speech to begin the festivities.

"Citizens of Oakview, thank you for attending this naming ceremony for a special new sandwich which will soon appear on the menu of the Sandwich Station. Your sense of community continues to amaze me when we come together for events such as this. And now, I will turn things over to the restaurant's owner, Archie Manfree."

"Hello, friends!" Archie bellowed as he looked about the Station at the tremendous crowd.

His apron du jour was a series of reminders in white on a navy blue background: "Smile," "Live Joyfully, "Laugh a Little Every Day."

Perhaps they were Archie's reminders to himself in this uncertain time.

He continued, "I would like to thank you for your overwhelming number of entries for the new sandwich, and I thank the Chamber of Commerce for choosing the top three names. Harley Keffer, Chamber president, will now announce the names. Please keep in mind that the first-place winner will receive vouchers for a free month of sandwiches, and the second- and third-place winners will receive a week's worth," he reminded the crowd.

"Drumroll, please!" Archie cried out as a drummer from the Bennington High School marching band played a single snare drum.

"Okay, everyone!" said Harley. "We had some great names to choose from, but here are the winners!"

"In third place, with the title of 'Gooey Gobler,' is Lexi Cassidy! Mayor Max, did you fix this vote?" he joked as Lexi came up to receive her prize. Everyone knew that Lexi was the biological mother of Mayor Max and Harley's son, EJ.

The crowd roared with laughter.

Harley continued, "In second place, with his entry of Tur-Bri-Bac, is Cooper Patterson! Just so you know, his mom, Jackie, recused herself from the voting because her sons entered the contest. Come on up, Cooper!"

Cooper bolted for the front of the Sandwich Station to collect his prize, a huge grin on his face.

"Mom, I did it!" he beamed as he handed Jackie his sandwich vouchers.

"Great job, Cooper! You get sandwiches for a whole week!"

Jackie just had to laugh. The ironic thing was that, if the Pattersons chose to, they could eat sandwiches from the Sandwich Station for 365 days a year. They just had to ask Uncle Archie!

"Now I have the privilege of announcing our first-place winner!" beamed Harley.

"In first place, with his entry entitled Butterball Bacon Bomb, is Jason Walters?"

Harley was stunned. His announcement became a question because he couldn't believe that Jason would participate in something as trivial as a sandwich naming contest.

There were no names attached to the list of entries that the Chamber voted on, so no one knew who entered the contest.

The audience was so surprised that they forgot to clap. Instead, they started to talk among themselves and stare as Jason came up to snatch his prize.

"I told you, Dad! I told you they'd pick your name!" Mikey started jumping up and down when Jason returned to him.

"Well, son, you were right! Start planning what kinds of sandwiches you want. We have 31 vouchers, but we have until the end of the year to use them," said Jason.

Just then, a reporter for the *Oakview Register* descended upon the Walterses, and started to pepper Jason with questions, and a photographer took snaps of the winners.

DJ PJ Panda from KFUNN played Queen's "We are the Champions" on his portable DJ station.

It was Jason's 15 minutes of fame.

It seemed as if the time between Archie's pronouncement about his prostate cancer surgery and the actual day of the surgery passed by in a flash.

Twenty fleeting days of worry, hope, and wondering.

Patsy had arrived two days before the surgery and her grandchildren were so pleased that she came to stay for a while. Her husband, James, had a golf tournament that week, so he was unable to make the journey.

Preceding the surgery were long talks with Patsy, pre-op testing, and a blowout pizza party at Jackie's the night before with her family, Patsy, Roger Meadows and Archie.

Patsy drove Archie to the hospital early in the morning; his procedure was slated for 9:00.

Arm-in-arm they entered Oakview General Hospital, Patsy's old stomping grounds when she worked an occasional shift there.

Jackie closed Treasures at noon and went directly to the hospital. Her children were instructed to go to daycare straightaway after school, so she had a few hours to devote to her BFF.

She sat between Patsy and Roger in the drab waiting room where other visitors waited anxiously for their loved ones and sat on uncomfortable plastic chairs.

The hours dragged on.

After playing many games of Angry Birds on her phone (Jackie), watching *The Kitchen* on the Food Network on his phone (Roger), and reading the latest edition of the *New England Journal of Medicine*

(Patsy), Archie's surgeon, Dr. Phillip Rivers, entered the waiting room.

Surprisingly, he wasn't familiar to Patsy.

"Are you relatives of Archie Manfree?" Dr. Rivers asked.

"Yes!" Patsy, Roger, and Jackie shouted at the surgeon concurrently, and they all stood up.

A white lie, but it was closer to the truth.

Archie was an only child who was asked to leave his Christian parents' home after he came out to them on his 21st birthday.

The Pattersons, Castleberrys and Roger were his only family.

"The surgery was successful. It was laparoscopic, utilizing robotic arms. We made several smaller incisions and used special long surgical tools to remove the prostate," the doctor said.

"Who will be caring for the patient?" he asked.

"We all will," said Patsy, "but I will be his chief caretaker when Jackie and Roger are at work." She pointed to the others.

"Okay, a nurse will come out and give you post-surgical instructions. Thank you all for caring for Archie. He will be in recovery for a few hours."

With that, Dr. Rivers took his leave.

And Patsy, Roger, and Jackie cried simultaneously, encircling one another as relief replaced the exhaustive hours that they had just endured.

Chapter Four

Harley called the Chamber of Commerce meeting to order. Held at Pizza Project #2, it was a special meeting planned spontaneously as Harley had important information to disseminate to the Chamber about some exciting news.

Those assembled chattered away, while many questions swirled around them.

Was there trouble with the city?

Was Harley stepping down as Chamber president?

Are our city's finances secure?

Harley put an abrupt end to their speculation as he stood before the crowd.

"Hello friends," he began, and glanced at the manager of PP #2. "Thank you, Debra, for hosting this unplanned meeting. And thank you all for coming."

There was an absence of goodies and coffee this time.

"A few weeks ago, I received a call from a producer at the Hallmark Channel, who informed me that, because of our charming little town, they are going to be filming a Christmas movie here on Main Street in May! That gives them two months to plan for the filming, and two months for us to prepare for the onslaught of actors, directors, producers, extras, and all of the accoutrements that come with a film shoot."

He continued, signaling to Gloria Sheffield, owner of the Hope Inn.

"Hallmark has already booked rooms at the Hope Inn and the Oakview Sheraton for two weeks, which is the approximate time that it takes to film their movies. And the company will be asking citizens of Oakview to apply to be extras, which is a paying gig," he declared.

"And some citizens will actually have small speaking roles, which pay even more."

The Chamber went wild. A lot of them wanted a piece of the action.

"Our town will be decorated for Christmas, as it will be a holiday movie. So, look forward to a Christmas celebration in May. I assume that there will be decorations all over Oakview," predicted Harley.

"So, Harley, will they be filming inside our stores? " asked Maisie, who incessantly fielded questions in her unending thirst for knowledge at every Chamber gathering.

"Gosh, Maisie, I really don't know. Mayor Max is reviewing the paperwork that Hallmark has presented to him. Within the next two months, we will learn a lot more about the movie shoot. You know what, everyone? We are so lucky to have a mayor who is also an attorney," declared Harley.

The entire Chamber nodded in agreement.

Patsy proved to be a godsend for everyone in Archie's healing circle. She stayed for a week at Jackie's, and everyone took turns caring for Archie.

On Patsy's last evening at Jackie's, the children asked to dine at the Sandwich Station. Archie's second-in-command, and present interim manager, Ross Beringer, was taking over for Archie for the next month. And Roger was with Archie.

One of the rules of post-prostate surgery was no heavy lifting, something that Archie did on a daily basis in the restaurant prior to surgery.

"Mom! We get to use four of my vouchers for sandwiches!" announced Cooper, who produced the crumbled vouchers from his pants pocket.

"Honey, thank you for treating us to dinner!" said Jackie as the foursome perused the sandwich board.

"What would you all like?" she asked the others.

"Well, I would like the French Dip au Jus Jus," said Patsy. "That sounds really good."

"I am going to try the Butterball Bacon Bomb, but without the cheese," said Riley. He wasn't so sure about brie cheese.

"I will have the Cheesy Grilled Cheese," said Cooper, whose mouth was already watering.

"And I am going to try the Butterball Bacon Bomb *with* cheese," said Jackie, intrigued by the newbie sandwich.

"Who wants chips or fries?" she asked the group, and also got their choices for soft drinks.

After the others bolted for a table, Jackie approached the counter and put her order in. While she waited, she spied Jason and Mikey coming in the front door.

Instinctively, she braced for the oncoming cold front in the form of Jason, and was glad that her food was ready.

Mikey ran up to her and hugged her.

"Mrs. Patterson! How are you all doing?" he asked as she was delivering food and drink to the table.

"Great! We are using some of Cooper's vouchers for our dinner. Mikey, this is my mother-in-law, Mrs. Castleberry." she pointed out Patsy.

"Nice to meet you, Mrs. Castleberry," said Mikey as he approached to shake her hand.

This kid is only 16, Jackie reminded herself.

Looking on from his place in line, Jason just scowled and looked away, as if the genial scene was abhorrent somehow.

"Mikey, are you getting sick of sandwiches yet?" asked Riley as he dug into his Butterball Bacon Bomb, minus the brie.

"I could never be sick of sandwiches!" declared Mikey, a wide grin on his face. "I have even thought of ditching my paper route and working here!"

"Wow, that is really cool!" said Cooper. "Then you could eat free every day of the week!"

The merriment was broken with Jason's pronouncement.

"Mikey, I need you to order," he barked, leading many in the restaurant to turn their heads and see who the loud barker was.

Looking embarrassed, Mikey said goodbye to the Pattersons and joined his dad in line.

"I see that nothing has changed with Jason Walters," said Patsy, nodding in his direction. "That man seems to have a permanent frown upon his face. He is too young to act like a curmudgeon. What a shame. What a shame."

Archie lived in a small bungalow a few blocks away from the Sandwich Station. When he wasn't showing houses for Homeland Realtors, Roger was by Archie's side, cooking for him and helping him to shower and groom. The two had met when Archie was looking for a home after acquiring his restaurant, and Jackie suggested Roger.

At the time, Roger was committed to his then-boyfriend, who ended up cheating on him. It was adios to Franklin soon thereafter.

"Roger, I am so grateful for all that you have done for me this past week," said Archie that evening at his bungalow. "I can never repay you for the time that you have devoted to me."

"Oh, Archie! I know that you would do the same for me, if the situations were reversed," Roger said emphatically.

Roger was moved to hug his GBFF, and then they did something that they had never done before. Suddenly, they were embracing, and a quick peck on the cheek wasn't enough.

They started kissing passionately, drawn to each other in Archie's time of need. It was as if their hunger was sated in their embrace.

All of the events of the past week had wrought in them myriad emotions: fear, anxiety, relief, hope, and, at this moment, pure joy.

They continued to kiss and explore each other's bodies and their love was sealed.

Maybe the Beatles were right all those years ago. Love *is* all you need.

Jackie had a moment to herself the next morning at Treasures after she and her children bade farewell to their precious Grandma Patsy, who had passed along the instructions for Archie's care to her and Roger.

She decided to read another love letter in the jewelry box and surreptitiously dipped into the box.

My dearest, dearest Margaret,

Tomorrow I catch a plane to California and end my time in the Peace Corps to focus on my reunion with you, my beloved.

Even though I have scolded myself on my feelings about joining the Corps, I am proud of all of the homes that we have built and the poor people that we have helped to become farmers while teaching them the basics of planting fruits and vegetables.

I leave here with a sense of fulfillment, despite my conflicted feelings.

I look forward to your meeting me on the tarmac of the Los Angeles International Airport tomorrow evening with my parents and your parents.

Yours ever,
Robby

She grabbed another letter, a PS to the one she just read.

PS,

I have learned so much about planting and harvesting fruits and vegetables, and I hope to plant many in the yard of our home when we become husband and wife.

If you'll have me.

Yours,
Robby

Jackie thought about how she would love to share the love-filled communications with Rachel, who was an incurable romantic. Rachel fell hard and fast, her crush on Patrick a testament to that fact.

In addition to her part-time job as a receptionist in a doctor's office, Rachel penned prolific romance novels and had a huge presence on social media. She kept the receptionist job to glean ideas for future novels by people-watching.

Every once in a while, Jackie would peruse Rachel's Facebook page, scanning her latest tomes and book signings, releasing a heavy sigh that her sweet sister was now gone from her life, but, hopefully, not forever.

Rachel was quite the writer, having penned ten novels already. She was an international author, and had book signings in England, France, and Spain.

Jackie would love to hear of Rachel's travels and adventures, but that was not meant to be. At least for now.

She replaced the letters, and, as she told Sabrina, it was her quest to find the recipient of the missives. She wouldn't stop until she did.

That evening, she asked her children what their roses and thorns were for the day. Over chicken nuggets and macaroni and cheese, Cooper and Riley shared their ups and downs.

"Well, Mom, I would say that saying goodbye to Grandma Patsy was a huge thorn for me. I just love her and her bag of tricks!" said Riley, a huge grin on his soon-to-be-six-year-old face.

"I know," consoled Jackie, as she cast a glance at both of her sons' downtrodden eyes. "But you will see Grandma Patsy very soon, I'm sure."

"What was your rose?" asked Jackie.

"Since you mentioned it the other day, I thought of where I want my birthday party to be! At the bowling alley!"

"Okay, the bowling alley it is!" Jackie feigned sincerity, but immediately began to worry about a bunch of kindergarteners with heavy balls in their hands.

"So, Cooper," she asked. "How about your rose and thorn?"

"I guess I have the same thorn that Riley does. I really love Grandma Patsy and I loved how she came to stay for a whole week. She is so smart, and she is always teaching us stuff when she visits," said Cooper.

"My rose from today," he added, "was that Mrs. Johnson said that I get to say the Pledge of Allegiance over the loudspeaker every day next week!"

"That's wonderful, Cooper!" exclaimed Jackie. "I will be there on Monday to read to Riley's class, so I will get to hear you over the loudspeaker!"

Little victories, Jackie thought to herself. Little victories.

Jackie decided to post a message on Facebook about Margaret and Robby. She included a partial picture of Robby's beautiful handwriting, and left a few clues about the contents of the letters.

Now, she just had to wait.

On Monday, she read Beth Ferry's *Swashby and the Sea* to the kinder bunch, delighting in the sound of Cooper's voice with the Pledge of Allegiance before class began.

The book was a hit with Miss Williams' class, who loved the tale of Captain Swashby, a retired sailor who lives a quiet life by the sea until an energetic girl and her grandmother move in next door. They change his grumpy perspective with their kindness.

During chat-time, Jackie asked the students about their neighbors and what they liked best about them.

Twenty hands shot up straight in the air.

"Mrs. Patterson," declared Trevor Jones, "there is an older boy in our neighborhood named Bobby who babysits us sometimes. He talks to his girlfriend on the phone *all the time*!"

The kindergarteners all laughed.

"Well, I guess that's quite common with teenagers," said Jackie, smiling and portending what was certain to happen to her boys in less than ten years.

She called on Piper Chapman.

"Mrs. Patterson, we have this really old guy on our block who just hates kids. We cross the street instead of passing by his house because he is so mean!"

Jackie shuddered, and immediately thought of Jason.

And wondered what all of the neighborhood kids thought of him.

Since she had some time to herself, Jackie texted Archie to see if he needed some lunch.

Hey there! How are you doing today? Want me to bring something for lunch? Maybe from the diner or China Place? You are probably sick of eating from your own restaurant!

Archie replied.

Girlfriend! What a marvelous idea! How about the Imperial Dinner at China Place? I'll have the hot and sour soup instead of the egg drop. And please bring enough place settings for three.
Thanks so much!
L & K

Archie concluded the letter with his signature *love and kisses.*

Jackie was intrigued. Roger must be the third person. He had to be.

There was a definitive shift in Archie and Roger's collective demeanor that Jackie noticed immediately as she entered the cottage. Their smiles were more robust and they were physically closer than they ever appeared, at least in Jackie's remembrance.

"Archie!" bellowed Jackie, careful to hug him. "You look wonderful! How are you feeling today?"

"Much better, honey. You know what? Dr. Rivers said that I can return to work next week! My good juju is back!"

He added robustly, "Hallelujah! Hallelujah!"

Roger joined in the hooting and hollering, as Jackie looked on.

Yup, something's going on here, she thought. Her next thought was how cute they are, if indeed they are a couple. Both gingers, like Mayor Max.

Maybe they can start a club: the Ginger Gay Men!

Chapter Five

Spring was leaving its prolific mark upon Oakview as blossoms appeared on jacaranda trees that dotted the city, their vibrant purple flowers popping. Though the oak was the more abundant of the two trees, it bowed to the jacaranda in its blue-violet grandeur.

As she drove to work and witnessed the jacarandas in their spring splendor, Jackie thought of a poem that she read in her English 101 class at Walker College: "[in Just-]" by E. E. Cummings.

Cummings describes the world as "mud-luscious" and "puddle-wonderful" in spring.

Perfect for today, she thought.

So far, Jackie had received no responses to her Facebook post regarding the lovers Margaret and Robby. Give it time, she reassured herself.

In advance of Riley's birthday bash, Jackie had created invitations to his whole class and enlisted the (paid) help of Mikey and (unpaid) assistance of Archie, who was taking it slowly and careful not to lift anything beyond 10 pounds.

Jackie had rented a room at the Smashing Pins bowling alley, and ordered pizza and soft drinks. A huge sheet cake with a horse theme awaited cutting on a table in the room.

As the youngsters filed in, Archie readied himself for the onslaught and for the inevitable query from Jackie. He wasn't too comfortable around a group of children, and he knew that, given the opportunity, Jackie would pepper him with questions.

"Okay, Archie. You can do this. And when the last kid leaves, I want you to come over to my house for a long talk and a glass of wine. Deal?" asked Jackie.

"Deal!" echoed Archie.

Surprisingly, there were few snafus in the 90-minute party.

After pizza, the group split up and filed into three lanes, laughing and competing for first place.

Donovan Price, an inexperienced bowler, went to throw the ball and ended up halfway down the lane, splayed across the surface with the ball still in his hand.

And Sherry Clark, drinking fruit punch at the time of Donovan's display, was so shocked at the scene that instead of swallowing it, the punch came out of her nose. She dissolved into laughter, as did the rest of the partygoers.

When the party was blessedly over, Jackie paid Mikey $20 and drove him and her children home. Archie followed in his own car, as he was recently cleared to drive post-surgery.

Jackie's parents, Bill and Peggy Timmons, called to wish Riley a happy birthday. They were happily ensconced in the Florida Keys.

Riley, who didn't have a chance to open his presents at the party because of the time constraints, sat in a circle with his brother and opened them. Cooper jotted down who gave what, as Jackie was insistent on her sons' writing proper thank-you notes.

Since the boys were occupied, Archie and Jackie sat on her patio, wine in hand and snacks of cheese, crackers, and fruit on the table.

"So, do tell about you and your GBFF, my friend. I could tell that there were electric sparks flying between you and Roger when I visited your house," began Jackie.

"Oh, honey! We made a love connection!" exclaimed Archie as he grabbed a Wheat Thin and a mini slice of pepper jack cheese.

He continued, "Roger has been by my side when he hasn't been working. He has done so much for me. We became closer metaphorically before we became closer physically," he said.

"Oh," he said, punctuating his remarks with a wink in his eye, "I'll have you know that the little blue pill works wonders for me!"

Jackie just smiled, happy for her friend.

Everything was set in motion for the Hallmark movie. Rooms were booked at the Hope Inn, the Oakview Sheraton, and the Glendale Hilton for the cast and crew of *Christmas in My Hometown.*

Everyone was excited to see the throngs of movie people descend on the small town of Oakview, who all took in the sights of the city as soon as they were situated in their hotel rooms.

Because filming was going to take place all day and in the nighttime, school kids were tapped to be extras in the late afternoons and evenings.

And, because it will be a holiday movie, the film's creative director had adorned Main Street with holiday wreaths and garland, in addition to mounds and mounds of fake snow.

Fully adorned Christmas trees appeared in Main Street's shops and on the streets, and carolers lent their harmonies to Oakview and its citizens.

Lights and camera equipment were spread out over the town, with scaffolding for outdoor photo and video shoots.

As Harley mentioned to the Chamber, the premise of the movie revolves around a female protagonist (Stella Perkins, played by Jennifer Watkins) who is fired from her publicist job and returns to her hometown of Nevada City, California for the holidays.

While there, Stella becomes involved in the town's Christmas pageant as a favor to her parents and ends up in the emergency room when she falls off a ladder while putting up decorations in the high school gym.

The new town doctor in Nevada City, Preston Wiggs (Jonathan Edwards), ends up healing both Stella's ankle and her heart.

Footage was taken in many shops on Main Street, including Oakview Cleaners.

Though she initially questioned the presence of the *Hometown* crew, Maisie became instantly starstruck when Stella dropped off a dress for the Christmas ball.

Flustered, Maisie had to do five takes with her scant lines: "May I help you?" and "The dress will be ready by 5:00 tomorrow."

The film crew and the principal actor, Jennifer, were enchanted by Main Street Treasures: They requested that Jackie set out some Christmas items in the front of the store for the three days that they spent taking footage of the shops. And, between cast and crew, much of Treasures' inventory was snapped up during the two weeks of filming.

Jackie had to consult with Sabrina about obtaining additional items for the store.

Mikey was slated to play a patient named Jimmy Rollins in Dr. Wiggs' office, which was really a jerry-rigged conference room in the Oakview Sheraton. Jimmy suffered from a broken arm, a role that wasn't much of a stretch for Mikey.

Turned out that extras got paid $50 an hour, and those with a speaking part, like Mikey, were paid $100 an hour.

A fortune for a young man like Mikey!

Jackie and her children met Patsy and James for dinner at Walt's Diner. The couple had been visiting with Archie and Roger, checking up on Archie's health. They also dropped by and saw their two baby granddaughters.

"Grandma! Do you have your black bag with you? I want to hear your heartbeat!" queried Riley.

"Yes, sweetheart! It's in our car. I will get it for you," said Patsy, who is never without her infamous black bag.

Instead of getting her bag, Patsy produced a smaller kids' version, with a stethoscope that really worked.

Riley went nuts.

"Oh, Grandma! What a perfect gift for my birthday! Thank you, Grandma and Grandpa!"

He ran to hug James and Patsy fiercely.

"I knew you'd love it!" exclaimed Patsy.

Over dinner, Jackie filled Patsy and James in on the comings and goings in Oakview.

The couple was curious to learn about the progress of the Hallmark movie.

"Mikey got a job playing a patient in a doctor's office. The kids can't wait until the movie comes on television," Jackie said.

Cooper piped up.

"Grandma and Grandpa, Mikey is going to be a movie star!"

"Tell us about his role in the movie, Cooper," James requested.

"Well, he plays a boy with a broken arm," said Cooper, "which he had in real life a few months ago. At least he knows what it's like to have a broken arm."

"I should say!" said James.

Changing subjects, Patsy inquired about the upcoming Memorial Day holiday as they exited the diner.

"The elementary kids have off Friday through Monday," said Jackie, "which is odd, as the high school is only off Saturday through Monday."

"Well, how about if the boys come visit us that weekend? We can go to the beach and maybe hit Disneyland," said Patsy.

"Yes, yes, yes!" said Riley.

"Yeeessss!" echoed Cooper, as the boys started jumping up and down.

"Well, I guess that's settled!" Jackie concurred.

And she thought about the luscious bubble bath that awaited her on the near horizon.

Later that evening, Jackie got a Facebook message from someone named Jennifer Collins. The name did not ring the slightest bell.

Hello Jackie,

My aunt and uncle are Margaret and Robby, but my aunt goes by Maisie, and people often called my uncle Robert.

Maisie thought that her letters were lost forever and couldn't remember where she left them. I know that about six months ago she cleaned out a closet and gave some things to Sabrina on consignment. That must have been where the jewelry box went.

I know that you are familiar with my aunt, as she speaks so highly of you. She would be so pleased to have the letters back.

Thank you for returning them to her. If I didn't live in Michigan, I would do that myself.

Gratefully,
Jennifer Collins

Jackie was stunned, but felt such bereavement at the imminent loss of the letters that she had so enjoyed reading. They were like a dessert for her day as she embraced the story of Margaret and Robby and savored each word.

First thing in the morning, she greeted Maisie and passed the jewelry box to her with the bottom drawer ajar. Maisie quickly hugged Jackie while clutching the box.

"Thank you, Jackie. I will be forever grateful," she said.

"Robert was the love of my life—the one and only love of my life. We met at a dance at the YMCA when he was fresh out of high school and on his way to the Peace Corps in a matter of weeks. I had one more year of high school left."

She continued, wistfully, "We fell hard and fast for each other, perhaps because of the time constraints in advance of Robert's departure. Those two years that he was gone seemed like an eternity!

73

But we were never separated after that, in 50 years of marriage, until he passed away."

As Jackie exited the cleaners, she glanced back to see Maisie grasp the precious missives to her chest, fittingly heart-adjacent.

The Friday of Memorial Day weekend, Jackie dropped her children at Patsy and James's Marina Shores home; the couple would be returning them on Monday.

Jackie had a half day off because the summer part-timer that Sabrina hired had started at Treasures that day after three days of orientation. By noon, she and the children were off.

Upon her return to her home, Jackie decided to do some gardening out front. It was rather therapeutic, and she enjoyed the solace, sun, and tunes coming out of her cell phone.

At around 3:00, Jason bolted out of his house, arms flailing and panic-stricken. He ran straight across his lawn to the Pattersons' yard.

"Jackie! There is an active shooter incident at Bennington and the school is on lockdown! I got an alert on my phone," he said, gathering his thoughts as he continued.

"One of the freshman boys came late to school and started shooting at objects like desks and chairs randomly, but so far he has not hit any people. I need to go see if Mikey is okay!"

He knows my first name, thought Jackie for a half second before blurting out "I'm going with you!"

She quickly grabbed her purse and locked the front door and dashed next door. Jason had his car idling in his driveway.

At Bennington, chaos ensued. Panicked parents were herded into the gym, television cameras and news reporters blanketed the campus, and those lucky students who escaped the school embraced relieved love ones.

In the gym, Jackie did her best to console Jason, who kept pacing back and forth, running his hands through his hair and trying to wrap his head around the confusion.

"He's all I have, Jackie!" he exclaimed, his pained, handsome face displaying his sorrow and his fear, emotions Jackie had yet to perceive in her next-door neighbor. "I don't know what I would do if I lost him!"

Jason already lost his wife, thought Jackie; it was unimaginable to consider the loss of his only child.

School resource officers and Oakview police tried to provide information on the fluid situation while being incessantly hounded by loved ones.

The gym was a noisy place, and it seemed as if it had been hours since any information was disseminated to those waiting anxiously.

Some parents were in tears, and there were circles of concern, as people gathered to share what little information they had about the incident and the shooter.

Suddenly, a policeman grabbed a cheerleading megaphone and made an announcement.

"The shooter is in the front office currently," he said. "Our men are going in."

Temporary relief washed over Jason as a stinging thought occurred to him.

"Jackie, do you know the layout of Bennington? I think Mikey has an art class that is close to the front office," said Jason, fraught with new worries.

"Jason, I am a Bennington graduate. And yes, the art wing is very close to the office. But don't worry—the officer said that his men are going in soon."

Without a second thought, Jackie took Jason's hands and held them tightly as she led him to the bleachers. They two sat side by side.

She flashed back to her senior year when she did the same with her boyfriend Brett James at Bennie basketball games. Sadly, the couple parted in college, as she stayed in town and went to Walker College and he attended the University of Washington in Seattle.

"It's going to be okay, Jason," said Jackie softly. "It's going to be okay."

They continued to hold hands as the chaos whirled around them.

In the front office, Principal Cassie Patterson exited her office to find herself face to face with the shooter, Jeremy Atkins.

She froze when she spied the weapon.

Sweat was pouring down Jeremy's plump, pimply face and his breathing was labored. He raised the 45-caliber gun, pointing it straight to Cassie's head.

She tried to remember her active shooter training, where she and the other staff and faculty of Bennington were trained for three hours and where different scenarios were played out with actors portraying shooters and victims.

There was that acronym, she thought. What was it?

ALICE! She remembered what it stood for: alert, lockdown, inform, counter, evacuate.

Cassie's administrative assistant, Ellie Robbins, awaited the officers at the back door. Wide-eyed, she stared at the scene unfolding right there in the office.

Jeremy continued his stance as Cassie decided to confront him.

"What are you mad about, Jeremy? Why would you want to come to school and frighten everyone here, to say nothing of parents and loved ones who are anxiously waiting to see them?" Cassie asked, feeling her hands shaking and breaking out into a sweat herself.

"Mrs. Patterson, you just don't understand what it's like to be bullied. I am trying to get back at the kids who bully me," said Jeremy, tears suddenly finding their escape from saddened eyes.

"No, Jeremy, I don't understand bullying, as I was never bullied, thankfully. But I know that this is not the method to use to get back at the bullies. This is destructive behavior that is good for no one," said Cassie.

"Please give me the gun," she pleaded, with an arm outstretched.

"Please."

Now uncontrollably shaking, Jeremy couldn't focus on the gun with tears filling his eyes. The hand clutching the gun bobbed back and forth as he tried to focus and make his next move.

He nervously glanced around the room in search of police or school officers who inevitably would descend upon the scene.

Suddenly all of the best laid plans Jeremy concocted prior to his arrival at Bennington that day vanished and he handed the gun to Cassie, and flew into her arms.

"I am so, so sorry, Mrs. Patterson!" he exclaimed. "I didn't mean to hurt you."

Oakview police crashed through the office, and radioed to the announcer/officer in the gym.

"Ladies and gentlemen, the shooter has been apprehended and you are cleared to join your loved ones. The students will be coming here to meet you," cried the announcer.

Jason turned to Jackie and found himself in a huge embrace.

Suddenly, Jason's woodsy scent enveloped her as she was transported back to the Sweetheart Dance.

He clung to her in his relief, grateful that he had her support in the midst of such a horrific situation.

Chapter Six

The Chamber of Commerce convened after Memorial Day weekend, just as the Hallmark cast and crew were wrapping up *Christmas in My Hometown* by doing additional exterior shots of the buildings on Main Street.

It was almost June, and the humidity was increasing its impact on Oakviewites as temperatures suddenly soared. Flip flops and shorts were seen in abundance, and public pools were set to open June 1st.

Within two weeks, students would flee Easton Academy, Oakview Elementary School, Bennington High School, and Walker College and enjoy roughly three months of freedom from academia.

Harley called the meeting to order, this time at Main Street Treasures, with coffee and goodies provided by Sandy's Dandies.

"Good morning, everyone!" he began. "Thank you all for coming this morning. And thank you, Jackie and Sandy, for your hospitality and treats. We have much to discuss this morning."

Over coffee, blueberry scones and cinnamon-raisin muffins, the group debriefed on the active shooting incident and their own little bit of movie magic.

"I wanted you all to know that the Bennington shooter, Jeremy Atkins, has left the school and is enrolled in a juvenile court school in Mount Olive called Youth Leadership Academy," said Harley. "He will finish out his high school years there."

"I heard that Cassie did a great job of calming the shooter down," said Cassie's sister-in-law, Sabrina, who wasn't back to work yet, but still liked to join Chamber meetings.

"If you ask me, that is way too close for comfort," declared Jackie.

"Yes, but it's all behind us now," said Harley, pivoting to change the subject.

"How was the filming of *Christmas in My Hometown*? Anyone get on camera?" he asked.

"I got two lines in the movie, so I was paid $100 an hour," boasted Maisie, a broad smile across her face and a twinkle in her eye.

"The movie crew and Jennifer gobbled up a lot of my inventory," shared Jackie. "It was nice to make the sales, but Sabrina and I have a lot of shopping to do!"

She glanced at her sister-in-law, and they both laughed.

"The crew filmed me and EJ decorating the Christmas tree in our office," said Mayor Max. "Luckily, he wasn't running around, as usual!"

The group agreed that having the Hallmark people around put Oakview on the map, metaphorically speaking.

"I can't wait to watch this movie next December!" bellowed Archie. "We are all going to be famous!"

He discussed feeding lunch to the cast and crew every day during the two-week period. The diner, Pizza Projects #1 and #2, and Sandy's Dandies handled the other meals.

"I made enough money to go on a great vacation this summer!" he shared, secretly wondering where he and Roger would be visiting when their schedules allowed. Just the thought of getting away together warmed his heart.

After the group dissipated, all who were left were Archie and Jackie.

"How is everything going, Archie? How are you feeling these days?" asked Jackie as she cleared tables of their tablecloths and deposited cups and plates in the trash can.

"Just peachy!" said Archie enthusiastically. "I am feeling well, the restaurant is hopping, and Roger and I are a match made in heaven!"

With that, he touched his chest where his heart beat.

Jackie's boys had a great Memorial Day weekend as, apparently, Patsy and James spoiled them rotten, as grandparents are wont to do.

"We went to Disneyland and stayed at the Disneyland Hotel and the next day we went to Knott's Berry Farm!" squealed Cooper as Jackie was manning the barbecue on Memorial Day, after Patsy and James had dropped the boys off.

"It was so much fun!" blared Riley. "My favorite ride of all of them was the log ride at Knott's because it was such a hot day and we got wet!"

Not to be outdone, Cooper shouted, "My favorite ride was the Haunted Mansion because my favorite holiday is Halloween!"

"Mom, did you know that Knott's Berry Farm turns into Knott's Scary Farm at Halloween? That is what our tour guide told us," declared Riley. "Maybe we can go in October."

He continued, "And they have all of these things to eat that are made of boysenberries. Like syrup for pancakes, boysenberry pie, and even boysenberry ice cream! We had the ice cream after lunch, and it was delicious!"

All that Jackie could see before her eyes were invisible dollar signs, passing by exponentially with each of her boys' comments.

She was by no means poor, but her modest income and Patrick's pension could ill afford such a fabulous trip. She was so grateful for Patsy and James and their penchant for spoiling their grandchildren.

For the last time that school year, Jackie was slated to read to Cooper's second-grade class. She felt a bit sad, but reminded herself that there is always next year, when she can read to first- and third-graders.

And, who knows? Maybe one day she will dust off her teaching credential and teach elementary school full time.

She tucked that thought away, for now.

Mrs. Johnson requested that Jackie read *Second Grade Friends* by Miriam Cohen.

The plot revolves around Jason, the protagonist, and all of his adventures.

His seven-year-old life is filled with ups and downs and joys and frustrations. His ability to come through in a crisis provides teachable moments about how to cope when things don't go quite as we expect them to.

Through it all, Jason has his friends to rely on.

After reading the book, Jackie distributed some fancy gilded stationery to the class, and she asked them to write four sentences about their best friend in second grade and what they liked about him or her.

The title was "My Best Friend."

After about 20 minutes, Jackie asked for volunteers to read their stories aloud.

Billy Martin's hand shot up first.

He stood next to his desk, gathered his thoughts, and began reading:

"My Best Friend. My best friend is Cooper Patterson. He is a really good baseball player, and he is a pitcher. He is kind to everyone, especially me. And he loves his family."

With that, he took a seat and glanced at Jackie, who was suddenly tearful. He feared that he said something wrong.

"Very good, Billy. Thank you for sharing your thoughts about Cooper," she said, wiping her tears.

The students exchanged letters, and Jackie left the classroom with a heart full to bursting.

Alone in his home office, Jason took a tech break and thought about Jackie for the $1,000^{th}$ time in the two weeks since he had last seen her at Bennington.

She was there for him in his panicked time of need. She smelled heavenly—a fragrant combination of lavender and vanilla—and her touch was soft but firm as she clutched his hands.

He didn't want to let go.

Jason was concerned when one of Jackie's kids was chatting with Mikey when they were in the Walters' den. Mikey had asked the boys if they were going to sports camps in the summer, and Cooper said that they might not be able to afford it.

Since he was an accountant, Jason was acutely aware of finances, especially when it came to his clients. He hoped that Jackie was taken care of financially.

He had a surreptitious plan which he kept close to the vest—and to himself.

Jackie had opened up Treasures on a sunny June morning, the day before school was let out for the summer for students of Easton Academy.

She had mapped out summer plans with her boys the night before over dinner: They were to go to daycare at their school Tuesday through Friday, and hang out with Jackie on Saturdays until the shop closed at noon.

Sundays and Mondays were their adventure days.

"Mom, do you think we can go to sports camp this summer?" asked Riley over dinner.

"I'm afraid not, honey," said Jackie as she stole a glance at her two crestfallen children. "It's just too expensive."

She continued, "But we can have our adventure days and there is the family trip to Hawaii in August. How does that sound?"

There was no response from Cooper and Riley, who collectively lost their appetites.

And Jackie's heart broke in two.

Maisie was babysitting her granddaughter Olivia at the cleaners and decided to take a short break to bring Olivia over to visit with Jackie.

Now a year old, Olivia was a blue-eyed blonde moppet with endless energy. She loved her grandmother, whom she would call Mimi, and loved visiting the cleaners, especially when it entailed a trip to Treasures for a new book.

"Who do we have here?" asked Jackie as she spied the toddler. "Who is this big girl?"

Olivia ran toward Jackie for a quick hug, then bounded towards the book section, enchanted with the brightly covered array of children's tomes.

She picked out a huge Harry Potter book, but couldn't lift it. Jackie steered her towards the toddler section, and Olivia chose *Moo Baa La La La* by Sandra Boynton.

The teaser notes on the back cover mention that the book is a fun way to introduce babies to different animals and the sounds that they make. The colorful cover illustrates a cow, sheep, and three pigs to make the title sounds.

"Isn't that darling?" asked Maisie as she scooped up Olivia and the book and made her way to the check-out counter.

"Oh, you'll have fun with that one!" beamed Jackie. "We had the author in for a book signing a few Saturdays ago. She did all of the sounds while she read the book aloud. This place was crawling with little kids!"

"I wish I'd known about that one!" said Maisie. "I usually don't shop in town on the weekends, but I would come out for that."

"Well, I have another children's book author coming in August. I will give you all of the details via email."

"Thank you, dear!" With that, Maisie and Olivia made their leave. Break was over.

Jackie was dusting the shelves in the clothing section of Treasures when she got a call from an unknown person. She contemplated not answering it, but did anyway. It might be someone calling about her kids.

"Hello, Mrs. Patterson? This is Bill Reddick, football coach and athletic director at Bennington High School. I just wanted you to know that an anonymous donor paid for your sons to attend sports camps here in July. Cooper is all set for baseball camp, and Riley has been signed up for soccer," said Reddick.

"But, Mr. Reddick, who would do such a thing? Do you have the person's name so that I may thank him or her?" asked Jackie, dumbfounded.

"No, ma'am. The donor asked not to be identified. Camps start July 5, but you might want to drop by the athletic office here at Bennington prior to that to complete the paperwork. Your sons can go through health screenings at the same time," said Reddick.

"Thank you, Mr. Reddick. Cooper and Riley will be so happy," said Jackie, wondering whom the anonymous donor could be.

This was something she would have run by Rachel, her chief confidante next to Archie.

Because they were only 18 months apart, and with the exception of Rachel's brunette hair, people assumed that Jackie and Rachel were twins because they looked so alike. They were constantly together, partners in crime and best friends.

Until that fateful summer.

There were so many wonderful moments that Rachel missed out on these past ten years: Jackie and Patrick's wedding, the births of Cooper and Riley, their soccer and baseball games, and just being in the presence of family, especially at times like Christmas and Thanksgiving.

It was Rachel's choice—and Rachel's loss.

Just then, Archie bolted through the door. Today's offering was French onion soup and a steak panini. His apron du jour was burgundy with yellow writing, and stated, "Don't be afraid to take whisks." Under the writing was a wire whisk.

He took a side step left and another to the right.

"I am totally beside myself!" he stated, arms flailing wildly with the declaration.

"I know just where to take Roger on vacation! I am going to buy him a ticket to Maui for our family vacation! I ran this by Patsy and James, and they were all for it!"

"That's great, Archie! You already have your own room at the resort, and I say the more, the merrier. We will have so much fun!"

Jackie joined in the merriment and thoughts of snorkeling and windsurfing danced through her Maui-bound mind.

Again, she said a prayer of thanks for her parents-in-law, who were really her parents-in-heart.

She had something important to discuss with them, she reminded herself as she picked up the phone after Archie left.

Jason had been avoiding Jackie the past three weeks, but was secretly pleased about his magnanimous and anonymous gifting.

Her boys had run over to Mikey the day before with the news that they were going to summer sports camp. Mikey was happy for the news, as he had a temporary job the week of camp working in the concession stand.

He had quit his paper route and would soon be working part-time at the Sandwich Station, where he was already famous-adjacent because of his father's winning title of the Butterball Bacon Bomb sandwich.

Jason was proud of his hard-working son, and hoped that he, himself, was a role model for a strong work ethic.

He thought about a much-needed trip this summer—for both himself and Mikey.

Just as he was about to leave for the Oakview Gym for his noontime workout, Jackie met him at the front door.

"Hello," she began, not sure if she should call him by name. And not sure how to behave around him since the Bennington incident. "How are you doing?"

"Just fine," Jason curtly replied, slipping back into his curmudgeon persona.

"I just wanted to run something by you," Jackie said tentatively.

"I was wondering if you might allow Mikey to join the whole Patterson family on a trip to Maui next month. There are tons of people in the family, with lots of little ones, which I know Mikey likes most of all. My parents-in-law are paying for the trip, and they would like to extend an invitation to Mikey at their expense, as they know that Mikey is like my kids' older sibling. And maybe he can do a little babysitting," said Jackie, anxiously waiting for an answer.

"Gosh, I don't know," Jason warbled, trying to put his thoughts together. He ran his hand through his hair, just as he had done in the Bennington gym.

Jackie recognized that gesture as one of nervousness, after witnessing it firsthand in the midst of a crisis.

"That is a very generous offer on the part of Mr. and Mrs. Patterson, but I think I'll have to pass on it," Jason said, inexplicably. "Please thank them for me."

"Okay, I understand," said Jackie, but she really *didn't* understand. Mikey would be crushed if he found out.

She turned in the direction of her home, glad that she didn't mention anything to her boys.

Chapter Seven

Sports Camp Week, as Jackie dubbed it, brought all hands on deck as the mid-July sun shone on the campers. Thankfully, they were finished by 12:00 each day.

Monday Jackie was off, so there was no need to bring in the reinforcements. However, the reinforcements came out to play Tuesday through Friday in the form of Archie and Roger, the boys' honorary uncles.

Jackie had asked everyone with whom she was close if they were the anonymous donor for the sports camp fees, but no one fessed up.

Another challenge for her to resolve.

Jackie's overloaded calendar resembled a jigsaw puzzle, the pieces being played with each day of camp.

She dropped the boys off at Bennington in the morning, and she and Archie took their lunches alternately to do pick-up by noon, when the boys were set free.

Afternoons were spent either at Treasures, or with Roger, who took the boys to several open houses. They liked those adventures the best.

"Mom, Mom!" exclaimed Riley, "Today we got some hot dogs from Mikey's stand and went to a house that had a gigantic staircase up to the second floor!"

"And Uncle Roger let us dip our feet in the huge pool and feed the fish in the koip pond!" bellowed Cooper.

Jackie laughed.

"I think it's called a koi pond, honey. I am so glad that Uncle Roger is taking you with him as he shows houses," said Jackie as she prepared lasagna for dinner.

"Mom, I have a question. Are Uncle Archie and Uncle Roger gay?" asked the older, wiser Cooper, eyebrows raised in questioning. "Billy Francis has a brother who is gay because he has a boyfriend. I've seen them pick Billy up from school."

Jackie froze and mentally addressed an ever-present ghost.

"Damn it, Patrick! You were supposed to be here to answer the tough questions along with me. We were a team, damn you!"

She quickly composed herself.

Get a grip, get a grip.

"Well, honey, there are a lot of different types of relationships in this world. There is the man and woman relationship, man and man relationship, and woman and woman relationship. Yes, your uncles are gay, because they are in a man and man relationship," admitted Jackie.

"Does being around them make us gay? Because I really like Samantha Jones," fretted Cooper.

"Oh, no, honey! You decide for yourself what kind of relationship you like," said Jackie.

Pivoting, she asked, "Tell me about Samantha. What's she like?"

And sort of dodged a glossed-over bullet.

Harley called the Chamber of Commerce meeting to order on a sultry August morning as Oakview was already bathed in mugginess at 8:00 in the morning. Today, the meeting was held at the offices of Maxwell Dunlap and Associates.

Little EJ, 3, was running around the bank, and Max was trying to corral the toddler. EJ's sister, 11-month-old Sarah, was sleeping in a playpen in the "kiddie room," a glassed-in room adjacent to Max's office.

One of his part-time administrative assistants/babysitters wasn't due until 9:00.

"Good morning, everyone!" exclaimed Harley. "Thank you for your attendance this morning. Let's get started with our agenda."

The director of the Hallmark movie had informed Harley that the premiere of *Christmas in My Hometown* would be aired on Saturday, December 12.

"The executive producer of the movie will be on hand that evening to present a plaque to the citizens of Oakview," declared Harley.

"I think that we need to have a community watch party. What are your thoughts?"

"I know! I know!" bellowed Archie, his hand darting in the air like an eager schoolboy with the perfect answer. "Why don't we have the watch party in the Bennington gym? That's the biggest building in the whole town."

He continued, his thoughts landing on a huge idea, "Perhaps we can get some food trucks before the showing. I know that Cassie Patterson, Bennington's principal, uses several food trucks for events such as Homecoming. We will make it a huge Oakview party!"

"Great idea, Archie!" seconded Harley.

The group continued the watch-party discussion, and moved on to other topics.

Archie was pleased that the community agreed with his suggestion.

He was ready for a party, alright.

Gus dropped off three packages to Treasures on Main Street that afternoon, and Jackie couldn't wait to open the boxes.

It was her own personal treasure hunt, her secret stash that made her so happy. Someday she would tell Sabrina about her penchant for Gus's deliveries.

Today, Jackie unearthed toddler girls' clothing, which Maisie should be alerted to, and snow globes for the Christmas season.

Jackie figured that Sabrina had begun to gather Christmas inventory.

What was in the third box had her fascinated: The box read "Bauble Ornaments."

Inside were rounded red and green ornaments adorned with glitter. One was fashioned into a peppermint candy, a few read "Baby's First Christmas," one said "To my Favorite Teacher," and some were plain.

Along with the plain ornaments were tubes of gold and silver glitter paint pens with instructions on how to personalize them.

Wow! Jackie thought of how customers would go wild over the personalized ornaments. She wasn't very crafty herself—perhaps she could find someone to take care of the artsy task.

She decided to ask Sabrina to order more plain ornaments and glitter pens. She mentally hatched a plan to host an ornament-making party on one of the Saturdays in November.

What a great way to begin the Christmas season!

Her thoughts turned to her imminent vacation, which lately has been in the forefront of her mind.

In two weeks, the entire Patterson clan would be off to Maui en masse.

For Jackie, that meant a total orchestration of her schedule, with two part-time employees and a now part-time Sabrina taking over for her.

There was clothing to buy for her boys and essentials such as suntan lotion and swim goggles.

And Patsy and James were holding a pre-vacation dinner to discuss the trip, a sort of "rules of the road." Jackie, her children, and their uncles were invited to spend the night, as always.

As she was sorting the children's new arrivals in the clothing section, Jackie thought of how Cooper and Riley would have loved to have Mikey along on the trip. She didn't dare tell them that Mikey was invited; their hearts would be as broken as hers was.

I hope that Jason realizes what his son is missing, thought Jackie.

Archie was walking on air in the Sandwich Station the week leading up to his vacation. Today his apron was black with a sunset punctuated by palm trees. It read "Aloha Y'all!"

He couldn't wait to share the island adventure with Roger.

Long walks in the sizzling sunset. Pool time with the little kids. Perhaps snorkeling or surfing. Pedicures in the spa.

The possibilities were endless! But the fun was doubled with his love by his side.

Archie was working the check-out desk when Jason entered the restaurant, decked out in gym attire, holding one of his sandwich vouchers. He had used 15 of them and had 16 left.

Damn, thought Archie, Jason obviously just had a workout, but he still looks mighty fine. Too bad he's straight. Not that I'm interested, he reminded himself.

"Jason, my man! How goes it?" asked Archie as he wiped his hands on his apron.

"Just fine, Archie. That's quite an apron. Are you Maui-bound with the Pattersons in August?"

"That I am!" enthused Archie, barely able to contain himself. "And Roger is coming, too. We will have gobs of fun!"

After he ordered the Roast Beef au Jus Jus, Jason asked, "When are you leaving, and where will you be staying in Maui?"

He hadn't gotten the entire scoop from Jackie after their very brief exchange a few weeks back.

"Well, we will be gone August 7-13, and will be staying at the Hyatt Regency Maui Resort and Spa. You wouldn't believe all of the amenities! Everything from horseback riding to snorkeling to surf lessons. Good times ahead for all!" Archie bellowed.

Jason felt a twinge of guilt when he thought of the fun that Mikey would have had with such a great family like the Pattersons. And having lots of adults and a nurse in the bunch sweetened the deal.

Perhaps there was another solution to his conundrum.

And his guilt.

The entire Patterson family—in addition to Archie and Roger—descended upon Patsy and James's house for dinner a few days before the vacation.

Over a feast of Chinese food—delivered by Wok Like a Man in Marina Shores—the crowd conversed excitedly about their Maui stay.

James had prepared a Keynote slide show with dos and don'ts for the family, and addressed them after dinner.

"I am so glad that we are celebrating our *Wheel of Fortune* victory with all of you. This will be a wonderful vacation, but we have to keep some things in mind," James said as he made the presentation.

For the little ones, he reminded them to not swim alone, and to remain with their parents or another adult at all times.

For the adults, he reminded them to mind their p's and q's, which in old England meant pints and quarts. In other words, he cautioned them to watch their drinking.

Suntan lotion was a necessity for all, and he suggested that those who were going to partake in activities such as surfing and snorkeling should observe the buddy system.

"We will all have a great vacation together!" James commented as the crowd began applauding.

"Grandma, Grandma!" said Riley as he pulled the bottom of Patsy's shirt to get her attention.

"Yes, honey?"

"Will you be bringing your black bag to Maui?"

Riley put a great deal of thought into his questioning.

"Yes, I will, Riley. Do you know what? I think you should bring yours, too! You never know when someone will get stung by a jellyfish or get too sunburnt and need to be treated by you or me," said Patsy.

Riley beamed. "Okay, Grandma! I'll bring my black bag, too!"

Patsy smiled sweetly and her thoughts flashed to the future. Dr. Riley Patterson. She looked forward to seeing Riley's dreams come to fruition.

Chapter Eight

The glorious landscape of Maui was a welcome sight for the Patterson clan, exhausted after a five-hour plane ride. They rented six cars at the airport, bound for the hotel.

While the boys and their uncles were moving their luggage into the SUV that Jackie rented, Cooper and Riley bellowed simultaneously "Shotgun!"

Jackie's head began to throb, and Archie came to the rescue.

"I'm riding shotgun, you little rascals," he chided.

"Archie! Grownups don't have dibs on shotgun!" shouted Riley.

"Oh, yes, they do!" exclaimed Archie as he settled into the passenger's seat.

The boys sighed and acquiesced.

One for Uncle Archie, the peacemaker.

"Mom, did you know that there are seven pools that you find on the road to Hana?" asked Cooper as Jackie commandeered the SUV. Cooper had activated his iPad as they left Daniel K. Inouye International Airport.

"Tell us about it, Cooper," asked Roger, curious about a possible field trip with the bunch.

"Well, the description says that the seven sacred pools have magical waterfalls, and they are located in east Maui. They have places where you can buy a box lunch on the road. That sounds like so much fun!" Cooper enthused, wrapping up his Chamber of Commerce lecture.

"Honey, we need to go," said Archie, looking towards Jackie. "We could all use a little magic!"

He snapped his fingers and did a little car-dance.

"Okay, let's go in a few days, after we settle in," suggested Jackie as they entered the grounds of the hotel.

As they reached the Hyatt Regency, the sun was on fire—golden, orange, and red ablaze-- spreading out on the horizon.

Pristine white sand beaches reached as far as the eye could see, and the ocean proudly exhibited its hues of blue in abundance—from turquoise to teal to sapphire.

The atmosphere took the group's breath away.

James was the Hyatt greeter for the clan. He stood at the front door welcoming everyone who came through.

Jackie thought that James was probably a wonderful principal, as he naturally assumed a leadership role when the family gathered. He also was even-keeled, cool as a cucumber, and always in great spirits.

I'll guess retirement mellows a person, thought Jackie wistfully, as retirement for her was probably 20 years in the future.

The first few days of vacation were spent relaxing at the pool or beach. The more adventuresome of the clan chose to parasail, surf or snorkel.

A luau at the end of day two provided lots of fun for the clan: a dinner buffet highlighted by two giant roasted pigs, with background music provided by a Polynesian trio.

After dinner, Sabrina, Jackie, and Cassie learned the hula taught by costumed island dancers.

As the ladies took to the stage to dance, a sea of cell phones captured the hysterical moments as they apprehensively swayed to the music.

Capping the night were male luau dancers who performed a Samoan fire knife dance. The fire knife is a traditional Samoan cultural implement that is used in ceremonial dances. It is twirled, thrown, and caught by the dancer.

The audience oohed and aahed in amazement as the knives cut through the backdrop of the jet black sky.

As the group was headed towards the elevators après luau, Jackie suddenly stopped in her tracks. She couldn't believe who had arrived at their hotel.

Approaching the same elevators were Jason and Mikey, luggage in hand, looking spent from the journey.

"Mikey!" screamed Cooper as he tackled him, almost making him lose his balance and fall to the ground.

"Easy, Squirt! I'm glad to see you, too!" said Mikey as he glanced quizzically Jason's way.

Everyone was talking at once, as Jason approached Jackie away from the crowd.

"I felt guilty about saying no to sending Mikey with you, but I wanted to give him a nice vacation after all of his hard work in the classroom and with his paper route this year. I decided to come to Maui, as it sounded like a great trip. We won't be in your way," he promised.

"Oh, Jason, you don't have to make yourself scarce," said Jackie, instinctively touching his arm to make her point. "Just blend in with the rest of the clan. We won't care."

Jackie introduced Mikey and Jason to the bunch, and there was an overwhelming onslaught on the two.

Alone in her suite later, she tried to wrap her head around the fact that the two Walters men were here, in the very same hotel.

She didn't know if she was pleased—or fearful.

The next day, James, Patsy, Cooper, Riley, and their uncles set out on the road to Hana, and the Seven Sacred Pools.

Cooper shared more of his findings about the enchanted place.

"The Seven Sacred Pools are in a beautiful but very remote location, featuring waterfalls, freshwater pools, and incredible green foilage," he read from his iPad.

"Honey, I think the word is foliage, which means greenery, like trees," laughed Patsy. "Grandpa and I have been there a few times before, and it is absolutely beautiful."

Unfortunately, the group would only see three pools before someone got car sick.

Meanwhile, various members of the Patterson clan opted for a beach day, where they could take surfing lessons—among others--or just sit out and get their tan on.

Today, the ocean's brightest hue was emerald, and the sparkling water beckoned beachgoers to take a dip into its warm embrace.

Jackie, Cassie, and Sabrina chose to do some sunning, and had placed little Amelia and Rosalie in a portable crib equipped with an awning for protection from the sun. Their husbands were playing sand volleyball with other hotel guests.

From afar, Jackie saw Mikey carrying a surfboard and gave him a hearty wave.

"Oh, that must be Mikey's surfing instructor," she said, pointing out a very buff man, also clutching a surfboard.

"Uh, look closer, Jackie. I think that's Jason Walters, looking mighty yummy," said Sabrina.

"Yikes! You're right! I have never seen him shirtless before," said Jackie. "I guess all of those lunch breaks at Oakview Gym have paid off."

She couldn't stop staring at Jason, who was already sporting a bronze glow after just a day in the sun. His impressive physique had many on the beach turn their heads and take notice.

Her gaze followed Jason to the water, where he maneuvered the board like a pro and appeared to be giving surfing pointers to Mikey.

"Take a picture, it will last longer!" chided Cassie, using a childhood phrase.

The ladies laughed, and Jackie blushed.

"Ladies, I don't know what to make of Jason," admitted Jackie. "He is one big contradiction. His usual crabby side gives way to a sensitive side when he is vulnerable."

She reminded her sisters-in-law of the Bennington High School crisis, where she surmised that Jason was at his lowest emotionally.

"Well, he seems to be in good spirits here," commented Sabrina. "But even the crabbiest of people would be happy in Maui."

The conversation changed to recent Oakview news tidbits, a favorite topic among the women.

Word on the street is that Laney Prescott, editor of the *Oakview Register,* is engaged to Scott Williams, one of her writers.

And Veronica Hamilton, Maisie's honorary daughter-in-law, is pregnant with her second child, according to a very proud Maisie who marched over to Treasures with the fresh news before Jackie left on her vacation.

Also on the baby front: Debra Bertolli of Pizza Project #2 and her husband, Mario, have begun the adoption process. Each of them brought a child into their marriage a year ago. However, at 44 Debra is a tad beyond childbirth age, as some would attest.

But the juiciest piece of gossip was about Oakview's Chief of Police, Bryan Stanley, who is apparently dating the recently divorced Brenda Wilson, one of Glendale Police Department's 911 dispatchers.

"Bryan is such a nice guy, and as someone who has a very brief history of dating him, I think he would be a great catch," said Jackie. "I just hope he's happy."

"Why was your dating history brief?" asked Cassie, hoisting Rosalie out of the crib for a change.

"I was already beginning to have feelings toward Patrick when Bryan and I started dating, so I cut it off quickly, since it wasn't fair to him," Jackie admitted. "I think he was disappointed. Do you two know anything about Brenda Wilson?"

"I heard that she has three kids under the age of 10," said Sabrina. "That's a lot of kids to expose a bachelor to!"

Once again, Jackie thought of Rachel, who would have fit right in to the Patterson women's circle. She might even find fodder for her next romance novel.

The gossiping and Jackie's wistful musings were interrupted by Jackie's boys, fresh from the road to Hana.

"Mom! Mom!" yelled Riley. "We are back from our trip! We had to cut it short because Uncle Roger was feeling sick! But Grandma and I had our black bags and we gave him a cold towel to put on his face and neck, and we stopped and had lunch and he was feeling much, much better. Grandma told him to sit in the front seat on the way home."

Riley beamed at the news.

Already a mini-doctor, Jackie thought. Patrick would be so proud.

The next day, Jackie received a text on her cellphone:

Confirmed: Private horseback riding lessons at 2:00 for Jackie, Cooper, and Riley Patterson. Please report to Beckett Park across the street from the hotel. Your instructor will be Steve Hilliard, and the lesson will run for 90 minutes.

She was totally stunned! She didn't reserve horseback riding lessons! God only knows how expensive they would be.

Quickly, Jackie called Patsy and asked about the lessons.

"Patsy, I got a text that the boys and I are to report for horseback riding lessons this afternoon at 2:00 in the park. Did you arrange for the lessons?"

Jackie got the same feeling when she learned that someone had taken care of sports camp: confused, baffled, and very thankful.

"No honey, I didn't. But I know that the boys will be so happy, especially Riley!" declared Patsy.

It was a beautiful afternoon in Beckett Park as Jackie and her boys learned the basics about horseback riding and rode on the park's endless trails.

And it was a dream come true for Riley.

Steve Hilliard was very patient with the three of them and taught them the basics:

--Putting tack (accessories) on a horse

--Leading a horse on a rope

--Stopping and starting a horse

--Mounting a horse

The boys were exhausted that evening, but so excited to have this very cool and unexpected adventure.

"Mom, this was the absolute best day of my life!" declared Riley as Jackie tucked the boys in. "The absolute best!"

With that, he faded off to sleep.

Jackie was bound and determined to find her anonymous benefactor, yet again.

The vacation went by quickly, and the group gathered for their final luau the night before their departure.

There were no other snafus after Roger's motion sickness other than Pete's extreme sunburn after the volleyball game, which Patsy and Riley treated with aloe vera. Pete was fine by the next day.

Jackie's boys learned to boogie board and snorkel, and Jackie had some spa treatments with Archie and Roger while Cooper and Riley were at their lessons with other Patterson adults.

At the luau, Cassie, Sabrina, and Jackie once again entertained the crowd with their now-polished hula dancing, swaying to the beat of a quartet on ukulele, steel drum, recorder, and acoustic guitar.

Sunset provided the perfect backdrop for photos, and the entire Patterson family—plus Archie and Roger—took a group photo to record their island memories.

Archie was emotional after he and Roger took a couple picture with the glorious sunset behind them. He turned to Patsy with tears in his eyes.

"Oh, Mama P!" Archie exclaimed. "Maui has been the most magical place for Roger and me. We love walks on the beach, and trying a different tropical drink every day. And all of the fun activities and spa days. How can I ever thank you for this gift of the island?"

He turned to hug Patsy, who was getting teary-eyed herself, caught up in the familiar sights and sounds of her favorite place on earth.

During dinner, Jason and Mikey were on the way to their assigned table when Sabrina summoned them to the Patterson's huge family-style feast and two empty chairs. Mikey chose one next to Cooper, and Jason chose one between Jackie and Pete.

Jackie was thankful that it was nighttime, as she felt a blush creep over her face as she caught a whiff of Jason's now-familiar woodsy scent. He was so close to her that he must have heard her breath hitch when he sat down.

James greeted the group, as always, and offered a toast.

"Patsy and I would like to thank you all for taking this wonderful trip with us. And thank you, *Wheel of Fortune*, for bringing us here!"

Everyone laughed, glasses raised.

"I would like everyone to share what their favorite Maui memory was," he suggested, as family members went around the table, mentioning swimming, snorkeling, the luaus, and all of the other activities that the trip offered.

When it was Mikey's turn, he said, "I had no idea that we were coming to the same place as all of the Patterson family, but I am glad we did. Thank you, Dad, for this great vacation."

Jason smiled, so proud of his son. When it was his turn, he scanned the table, full of tan-skinned people who were happy to have shared this trip with the Walters men.

Finally, he said, "This vacation has meant the world to Mikey and me, and I am thankful that you have allowed us to join with you in your activities and meals. Your family is so special, and the love you all share is infectious. Thank you for allowing us to be part of that love."

He grabbed Jackie's hand and held it tightly, not caring if anyone noticed.

Chapter Nine

Maui was in the rear-view mirror two weeks later when students returned to Easton Academy, Oakview Elementary, Bennington High, and Walker College.

A hush fell over Main Street as tourists had vanished and Oakviewites assumed their autumnal routines.

Riley and Cooper were ensconced in first and third grades, respectively, and Jackie was back to her usual shift at Main Street Treasures.

Just as she was opening up the store, Archie came running over from the Sandwich Station. Today, his bright red apron bore the saying: "An apron is just a cape on backwards."

In his haste, he had no soup offering.

"Jackie! Jackie! Someone broke into my restaurant overnight! I used the police gizmo but no cops have arrived yet!"

"Archie, I am so sorry. What did they take?" inquired Jackie, fearful for not only Archie, but for herself. She accompanied Archie over to his restaurant after locking Treasures' front door.

"That's the weird part. I think they made a sandwich or two, and then left. Nothing of value was taken," informed Archie.

Just then, Bryan Stanley arrived on the scene, and Jackie returned to Treasures, looking quizzical at the disruption.

Mid-morning, Patsy called Jackie with some news.

"Hi honey," Patsy said. "I have something to tell you."

From the tone, Jackie could feel the concern in Patsy's voice.

"I went online to pay the boys' tuition for the first semester at Easton, and someone had already paid it!" declared Patsy, flummoxed at the discovery.

"Well, who would do such a thing?" asked Jackie, completely stunned.

Then she remembered the anonymous sports camp benefactor who was, presumably, also the horseback riding lesson benefactor.

"Patsy, I think it must be the same person who anonymously paid for Cooper and Riley's sports camps and horseback riding lessons," declared Jackie.

"That person is awfully generous," said Patsy.

Another mystery for Jackie to solve.

Gus delivered three packages in the afternoon, and Jackie delighted in this new treasure hunt. When Sabrina came back to work before the Maui trip, Jackie confessed that she loved getting new packages.

"Then I won't tell you ahead of time what I order!" Sabrina said, getting in on the treasure-hunt fun.

Today's booty consisted of additional green and red ornaments with glitter pens, Christmas kitchen towels in plaid red and white, and different snow globes reflecting the Oakview town square.

Jackie gasped aloud when she saw the snow globes. Whoever crafted them captured the town beautifully, with holiday lights strewn on the gazebo in the square.

Rounding out the scene were miniature carolers and Santa with a little girl on his lap and other children lined up to visit him.

It was a perfect representation of Oakview and its citizens.

"These will sell like hotcakes!" she said aloud, just as Jason came through the front door.

"Hello, Jason. I was just admiring a new shipment that came today. Look," she said excitedly as she held up the show globe and shook it.

"Those *will* sell like hotcakes!" Jason agreed, marveling, too, at the town resemblance.

119

Then he turned to Jackie.

"I would like to apologize to you, for all of the times that I was mean to you in my grief over losing Elisabeth. I was so mad at the world, and I was mad at myself. The trip to Maui reminded me of how precious life is, and kindness shouldn't be taken for granted," he said.

He continued, "Thank you for your kindness to both me and Mikey. You are a wonderful person and a wonderful mother. And you are like a second mother to Mikey."

Jason was moved to embrace Jackie, and she responded in kind, holding onto him tightly.

She once again completely forgot her "Jason mantra" and reveled in the touch of the man next door, who hugged her for a long time before facing her and pressing his lips to hers.

Such spontaneity and joy Jason had never known.

Just then, Archie opened Treasures' door and stopped short before closing it gently.

He just smiled and returned to the Sandwich Station, happy for his SBFF.

In reviewing the restaurant's surveillance tapes the next day with Chief Stanley, Archie discovered that two teenaged boys had broken into the Sandwich Station and helped themselves to a midnight meal.

The little scoundrels dismantled the alarm system before digging into huge sandwiches, chips, and bottles of Coke.

Bryan immediately recognized them and dispatched two of his men to their homes. As a punishment, the boys were to wash dishes at the Sandwich Station the following weekend for four hours each day.

"At least we know that those gizmos work!" enthused Archie, who felt a sigh of relief in having one.

He brought some chili and cornbread to Jackie when he had a lull in customers, along with his many questions.

"Archie, thanks!" said Jackie, whose mouth watered at the culinary present. She had skipped breakfast.

"Girlfriend, I have a big, fat confession to make," Archie stated, though he sported a huge smile on his lips and donned a purple apron that stated: "Miles of Smiles."

"I came over here yesterday, opened the front door, and saw you and Jason in a huge lip lock! Sparks were flying everywhere!"

Archie pointed his fingers in every direction and did a little dance.

"Archie! I can't believe you came over just at that moment! That was completely unexpected, believe me!" Blushing, Jackie then tried to explain the love connection.

"Well, whatever it was, it looked like mighty good juju!" exclaimed Archie.

"I am still puzzled at Jason's behavior," confessed Jackie. "He seems to be mellowing out, and the Maui trip appears to have softened him."

"Well, girlfriend, it is about time!" proclaimed Archie.

There was a measure of comfort—and sudden butterflies—in hearing Archie's pronouncement.

In her hotel room in San Diego, 90 miles from Oakview, Rachel Timmons plopped herself on the bed and let her long curly brunette hair fan out over the duvet.

She was exhausted after back-to-back book signings, this time promoting her tenth romantic tome, *Before There Was You and Me.*

Book sales were booming as Rachel began garnering tons of readers based on her reputation as a *New York Times* best-selling author.

She had done dozens of radio and television interviews, but was always glad to return to her Northern California home of Redding, the place where she landed after fleeing Oakview and her blistered feelings.

Rachel carved a place for herself in the Shasta County town, 120 miles south of California's northern border with Oregon. She worked part-time in the offices of John Spencer, MD, an internist, manning the front desk with two other employees.

She loved Redding and the condo community where she lived. It was a place for her to heal after fleeing Oakview in the wake of her broken heart.

Currently, she was single, but she did have a relationship for three years with Brad Covington, a patient of Dr. Spencer's. Although he broke up with Rachel in pursuit of another woman, they were friendly in the doctor's office.

Ironically, Rachel belonged to the condo book club, but there was one cardinal rule: Their monthly meetings would not feature any of her romance novels.

As the head of the book club, which was held in the condo rec room, Rachel devised that rule, as she wanted to expose her friends to various other authors.

A local celebrity, Rachel shares her books with the community, often reading to crowds at Happy Acres Convalescent Home.

And at the yearly silent auction for Redding High School, she offers all of her books, coupled with lunch with her, as a prize.

Currently, Rachel was on a week-long vacation in San Diego and would return to work on Monday.

She contemplated quitting her day job, as she was spending more and more time on the road. She had hired someone to manage her social media accounts, which kept growing with each published book.

Just as she did at least once a day, Rachel thought about Jackie, and the inevitable questions haunted her mind.

Were Jackie and Patrick still married?

Did they have kids?

Did Jackie work? Or is she a stay-at-home mom?

Did Jackie miss me as much as I miss her?

Though Rachel could find answers to these questions by contacting someone from her Oakview past, she chose not to. It was just too painful to contemplate what might be uncovered.

One day, she would return to her hometown and face her wonderful sister and slough off her selfish estrangement.

Just not today.

Jackie was anxious to hear all about the boys' first day of school. They looked exhausted at dinner, and she declared that baths would be in the morning, not tonight. An early bedtime was surely on the horizon.

Cooper was excited to share all about the new math book.

"Mom! I looked ahead in the new math book, and I understood the lessons! I loooovvve math!" he enthused.

"That's great, honey!" said Jackie, secretly hiding the fact that Cooper got his math knowledge from his father, not her.

In fourth grade, she couldn't understand long division to save her soul, and her parents had to hire a student tutor. From then on, she had what she termed a "math blockage."

"What about you, Riley? What's good about first grade?" she enquired.

"Well," declared Riley, "We are going to be learning all about the Presidents of the United States! I already know about George Washington and Abraham Lincoln, but I have a lot more Presidents to learn."

"Yes, Riley, you do. Good thing that you like history," declared Jackie.

When both boys kept nodding off while watching television, Jackie nudged them and marched them upstairs.

She decided to enjoy her tea on the patio, as the evening was balmy and the stars shone overhead, punctuating the velvet black sky with their twinkling.

Soon, the autumnal changes would add a briskness to the breeze, but for now it was warm, calm, and inviting.

Jackie's solace was broken by a familiar intruder: next-door neighbor Jason, who popped up above the fence to greet her after stepping on a picnic bench.

"Good evening, Jackie," he said. "Are you wishing on the beautiful stars tonight?"

Jackie laughed.

"Just enjoying their splendor," she said. "It's a gorgeous night."

"That it is," Jason agreed.

And had a sudden thought, perhaps prompted by the romantic starlit moment.

"Jackie, would you like to go out to dinner on Saturday night? I know that Mikey is available to babysit," he enquired.

"Oh!" Jackie was taken aback, and quickly gathered her thoughts.

"Sure, Jason. What do you have in mind?" She was curious about his intentions.

"Well, I thought that we would go to Primavera, since we are within walking distance of it," said Jason.

"Sounds great!" Jackie loved Italian food, and Primavera was an excellent restaurant.

On Saturday evening, Jackie had taken a long bath while her kids were watching a Disney movie after dinner.

She tried on three outfits before deciding on a vibrant sundress in primary colors and strappy yellow sandals. Perfect for a summer evening.

Jason and Mikey arrived promptly at 7:00, and Jackie gave Mikey instructions.

The kids had already had dinner, so they could have an ice cream novelty—just one!—for dessert. The garage refrigerator was full of ice cream sandwiches, Drumsticks, and orange Creamsicles.

If Mikey could swing it before the kids conked out, he should have them brush their teeth. They knew where the toothbrushes were.

Bedtime for Cooper and Riley was 9:00 on Saturday night, so he should adhere to that.

This wasn't Mikey's first time babysitting the kids, but Jackie was uncharacteristically nervous this time.

In fact, she was nervous about her dress, her hair, her perfume, everything!

This date mattered.

All of the times that Jackie and Jason were physically close swirled around her in happy memory: the Sweetheart Dance, Bennington, Maui, and Treasures were a kaleidoscope in her mind, as she looked forward to adding tonight to her list of intimate moments with him.

After instructions to Mikey and her kids, Jackie set off on her date with Jason.

Hand in hand, they traversed Browning Street to Primavera, one of Main Street's bright spots.

Gina Toledo, Primavera's owner, greeted them in her requisite green apron with a flag of Italy at the top of it, and led them to a quiet table in a corner of the restaurant.

Jackie laughed to herself, thinking that Archie probably would be apron-envious of Gina!

Over antipasto salads, plates of ravioli, and glasses of Pinot Noir, Jackie and Jason chatted comfortably. Their topics ran the gamut of the new school year, Main Street Treasures, and Jason's company, Oakview Accounting.

Jackie learned that Jason had attended San Diego State University, and, obviously, was an accounting major. He was a member of the Alpha Epsilon Pi fraternity and became its president his senior year.

Before landing at Oakview Accounting, he had a job traveling with the Los Angeles Rams, who were known as the St. Louis Rams at the time, handling all of the finances, from organizing hotel stays to plane flights and dinners out.

"Boy, the stories I could tell!" Jason bellowed. "Like the time after the Rams' Super Bowl championship over the Tennessee Titans when I had to fish two players out of a fountain at a hotel in Atlanta. They were drunk as skunks!"

He continued, "And the time that I got to perform the coin toss before a game as an honorary referee.   It was even televised!   Good times!"

If he had stayed with the Rams, he probably would have been the CFO, but he moved on.

He and Elisabeth decided to settle in Oakview after they got married.   Elisabeth was a pre-school teacher before she got sick.

Jackie shared about her college years, and the complicated relationship between Rachel and Patrick that caused Rachel to bolt.

But she quickly changed to subject to more positives in her life: her boys, her job, and the family she cherished.

When their spumoni ice cream was set before them, Jackie glanced at her watch.

It was 11:00!

They decided to get the ice cream to go, and set out on their walk home after Jason paid the bill.

Upon their arrival at the Patterson house, Jackie and Jason spotted all three kids passed out on the den sofas. Jason lifted Jackie's kids one at a time and brought them upstairs, and he tapped on Mikey's arm, woke him and Jackie handed him $40 as they walked out the door.

Planting a quick kiss on her lips, Jason made a promise to Jackie:

"Soon, Jackie. Soon."

She understood the implication.

Perfectly.

Chapter Ten

Harley called the Chamber of Commerce to order this first week of October at Oakview Cleaners. Maisie played hostess and Sandy brought goodies and coffee to the meeting.

On the meeting's agenda were the Autumn Festival and Christmas Extravaganza, two of Oakview's most cherished events.

"Okay, friends! Let's begin our meeting," said Harley, as the Chamber settled down at Oakview Cleaners.

Archie was the first to speak up when the Autumn Festival was mentioned.

"Happy fall, y'all!" he said, pointing to his apron adorned with fall leaves.

"Can you give Brenda and me a little run-down on the Autumn Festival, since we are the Main Street newbies?" he inquired and cast a glance at Brenda Finch of Two Scoops of Happiness.

"Sure," said Harley. "Well, the Autumn Festival is a weekend-long celebration that takes place just before Halloween. Main Street is closed down for the week, and booths are set up for vendors who wish to sell their goods. It could be anything, such as baked goods or clothing or jewelry. Also, there are small rides for the kids, including a petting zoo and a train."

He continued, "I have contacted the vendors from last year, and they are all on board. If you wish to set up a booth, please see one of Mayor Max's administrative assistants for the paperwork. Unlike other events where the proceeds go towards the Boys and Girls Club and Oakview Senior Center, the vendors will get the profits."

"Sounds like so much fun!" bellowed Archie, already thinking of the types of soup and sandwiches he will sell at the event. He'd ask Roger to help him and have his reinforcements man the Sandwich Station.

"It's a blast!" chimed in Sabrina, who was taking the first shift today before Jackie comes in at noon. "We also have bobbing for apples, which the kids love. This is a very kid-centric event."

The rest of the agenda was discussed before Harley called an end to the meeting at 8:30.

Jackie had an appointment for a mammogram at 9:00, and after the exam the technician asked her to get dressed and informed her that the doctor would be seeing her.

She was immediately fearful. Because of calcification on her right breast, she had been having mammograms every six months the past year and a half while the doctors monitored any changes to the abnormality.

Dr. Susan Collins entered the exam room.

"Hello, Jackie. As you know, we have been keeping an eye on the calcification, and, instead of just speculating about it, I think that you need to have a breast biopsy. It is an outpatient procedure, but you will need to have a driver take you there."

She continued, "A nurse will be bringing in some paperwork which will explain the procedure. And you can call the Imaging Center for an appointment."

"Do you have any questions, Jackie?"

"No, thank you. I will ask the nurse if I do," said Jackie, frozen at the prospect of having a needle cut through her breast.

She addressed her ghost again.

"Patrick, what will I do?" she pleaded. "You were supposed to be here in times like this, when I needed you the most!"

"You, too, Rachel!" she scolded her other ghost. "You both have abandoned me!"

Just then, a nurse named Barbara entered the room and explained that the procedure would be a stereotactic breast biopsy.

"This is a non-surgical method of assessing a breast abnormality and is performed by a specially trained radiologist. A local anesthetic is used, and there is a very small incision in the breast," Barbara explained.

Jackie left Oakview Medical Center in a haze, praying that the procedure would garner a negative prognosis.

She went home and called her parents, the Imaging Center, and then Patsy, and gave her the news.

"Oh, Patsy, I am so frightened!" Jackie intense fear was palpable.

"Honey, you will be okay. What I would like to do is to be in the room when your procedure is done, if that is all right with you. I know the head technician at the Imagining Center. Jane Bradley has done my mammograms for years," explained Patsy.

"Patsy, that would be such a comfort to me!" said Jackie. "You are like a guardian angel to many people, especially to Archie and me!"

It was all set: Jackie's procedure would be a week from Friday. Sabrina gave her the day off when Jackie saw her later in the day and informed her about the biopsy.

Everything was ready, but Jackie's apprehension was constantly tapping at her heart.

Jackie tried to find a way to inform her children about the procedure at dinner that evening. She thought all day about how to ease into the discussion without scaring them.

"Boys, I have something to tell you," she said tentatively. "Next Friday I am going to a special doctor and Grandma Patsy will be with me. I have asked Uncle Roger to pick you up from school that day, because Uncle Archie will be with Grandma and me."

"Are you sick, Mom?" asked Cooper, his eyes suddenly tearing up as he came around the table for a hug.

"No, honey, I'm not. The doctor just wants to use an X-ray to look into my right breast to see if there is a problem," Jackie tried to explain as simply as she could.

"Mom, do you need me and my black bag when you have this done? You know I can help with anything you need," offered Riley.

Jackie burst into tears at her precious children, so sensitive and caring.

They all enjoyed a group hug and returned to their meals, but Jackie had no appetite. Speculation did that to her.

Archie was especially protective of Jackie in the days leading up to the biopsy. He brought his daily offering of soup, sometimes with a sandwich or garlic bread.

And he tried to remain upbeat when he, too, was extremely fearful.

He popped in with bean with bacon soup and a miniature French loaf on Wednesday before the surgery.

His blue apron read "Caution! Hot stove! Hot chef!" Caution tape ran across the top of the apron.

Jackie just laughed when she read the apron.

"Archie, someone is making a killing on your apron fetish! How many of those do you think you have?" she enquired.

"Oh, in the neighborhood of 40 or 50," he said. "The customers just love them!"

He turned serious in the next moment.

"How ya doing, honey? How are you feeling?" he asked, concern covering his face.

"Archie, I am feeling like you felt before your prostate surgery. I am fearful of the future," Jackie confessed.

"Well, honey, just look at me! Everything turned out well, and I got a fantastic boyfriend in the process!"

He had a thought: "Maybe the same can happen to you! Does Jason know about the biopsy?"

"No, I haven't seen him around, and I haven't dropped by his place. I am worried that if we ever get intimate, he won't find me attractive if I have to have a mastectomy," confessed Jackie.

"Girlfriend, just take one step at a time. By Monday, you should have the results of your test, then you can go on with life," said Archie, trying to comfort her as she comforted him.

"Archie, thank you for all of your support," said Jackie as she hugged her BFF.

"You were there for me, and I am here for you, honey. Plain and simple. That's what BFFs do," said Archie.

There was much needed comfort in his kind words.

Jackie tried to keep her mind occupied on Thursday. She was happy when Gus delivered three boxes mid-afternoon and delighted in opening them.

Though it was only October, she felt in the Christmas spirit as she uncovered Christmas placemats, tree skirts, and picture frames in the shape of ornaments.

Sabrina had told her that holiday items would be moved to the front of the store November 1st, Treasures' official start to the yuletide season.

She couldn't wait.

When she picked up her boys from daycare, Cooper handed her a box with a hand-lettered message reading "Good luck, Mrs. Patterson!"

She was perplexed.

"Mom! All of the kids in my class and Riley's class wrote you letters!" declared Cooper. "The teachers said that we could either write a good-luck message or we could write a joke to cheer you up."

Jackie remembered talking to Caroline Williams, the kindergarten teacher, about her procedure when the women were supervising the car line. Caroline was a 10-year breast cancer survivor.

They women bonded in their shared experiences.

"What a nice present!" beamed Jackie. "Let's read some over dinner tonight."

The boys hooted and hollered over the jokes. They found each of them nothing short of hysterical.

"Mom, where do horses go when they are sick?" asked Riley.

"Gosh, I don't know, honey," said Jackie.

"A HORSEpital!" declared Riley.

"Here's a good one," said Cooper. "What do you call a pig that does karate?"

After a pause, he answered his own question. "A pork chop!"

Jackie needed this lighthearted moment with her boys. When she was up to it, she would write thank-you notes to Miss Williams and Mrs. Johnson and include her thanks to the students.

A proper belly laugh is good for the soul, she thought, as she watched her boys in shear amusement.

On Friday, Patsy arrived at Jackie's house bright and early, and she drove the boys to school. They loved having Grandma Patsy with them, and instead of dropping them off, they asked if she would walk them to their classrooms.

They were proud of their Grandma, and it showed on their beaming faces.

Jackie had added Roger's name to her approved-to-pick-up list at Easton Academy; he would be picking up Cooper and Riley after school.

At 3:00, Patsy, Archie, and Jackie arrived at the Imaging Center. After saying goodbye to Archie, Jackie was prepped for the procedure, which, she was told, would last about 90 minutes.

What a blessing to have Patsy here, thought Jackie. Her presence meant so much at such a scary time.

Jane Bradley described the biopsy before it began and helped Jackie as she lay face-down on the bed, designed with a hole where the right breast would be placed.

Patsy stayed by her side the entire time, rubbing her back and offering kind words and greeting the doctor who came in perform the biopsy. Surprisingly, the procedure didn't take that long.

Jackie was asked to stay in the prone position until any bleeding stopped.

When Jane had things wrapped up, Jackie got dressed and then she had a post-biopsy mammogram.

She would know the results by Monday or Tuesday. In the meantime, Jackie was to take it easy for three days and not lift anything over 10 pounds.

As she and Patsy entered the waiting room of the Imaging Center, Archie stood to hug Jackie gingerly, and the three of them glanced at the door as Jason barreled right through it.

"Jackie! Jackie! Are you okay?" he asked, coming to a stop in front of the trio. "I went to visit you at Treasures and Sabrina said that you were here."

Then he remembered his manners.

"Patsy, Archie, nice to see you," he said, gathering his thoughts quickly.

"Jason, I am fine. I just had the biopsy and I am going home to rest. Thank you for coming here," she said.

"I'll stop by later," he said, and bade goodbye to everyone.

"Honey, I think you are going to be in good hands!" chided Archie.

"I think so, too," echoed Patsy, smiling at his declaration.

When Jackie was alone an hour later, Jason came over with some dinner. Mikey had already had his hamburger, and Jason brought some for him and Jackie, along with some homemade French fries. He knew that Roger would be taking the boys to dinner.

"Oh, Jason! How thoughtful of you! I had no idea what I would eat for dinner, and I had no energy to cook anything. What a godsend!" Jackie exclaimed.

"Well, I wondered what you'd be doing, and I knew that the boys were out. Let's sit at the dining table and we can catch up," Jason said.

Once again, conversation came easily for the two. Wanting to keep it light, Jason talked about one of his co-workers who wasn't wearing pants on a Zoom call.

"I think he learned really quickly about camera angles!" he chuckled.

He also asked her if she wanted to go to the Autumn Festival, just a week away. He suggested that they bring the children.

"Jason, that would be just lovely! Thank you," said Jackie.

"Hey, I have a plan," said Jason. "Why don't I have the boys sleep over tonight, so you can have some me time and get your rest," he suggested. "I have twin beds in my third bedroom."

As if on cue, the boys came running into the house, Roger bringing up the rear.

"Mom! Mom!" yelled Riley. "Is everything okay? Do you need my black bag?"

"Oh, honey, I am just fine, thank you. And thank you, Roger, for picking the boys up and taking them to dinner," she said, reaching her hand out for him.

"We had a great time! They each ate chicken nuggets at the diner and we went to Two Scoops of Happiness for an ice-cream cone," said Roger.

He added, "Do you need anything before I go?"

"Oh, no," said Jackie. "You have already done so much for me."

The boys said thank you and goodbye, and Roger made his exit.

"Boys, Mr. Walters suggested that you spend the night at his house tonight," said Jackie, who was met with screaming kids.

"Yes, yes, yes!" replied Cooper.

"Okay, here are the rules," Jackie said. "No more dessert for tonight, and you need to brush your teeth before you go to bed. And bedtime is 9:00 on the weekends, as you know. Go get your backpacks, pajamas, and toothbrushes."

Jason picked up the dishes and placed them in the sink.

Out of sight of the boys, he bent down and kissed Jackie.

"Have a good night, Jackie. Rest your thoughts and your body, and know that soon we will do more than kiss. That is a promise."

With that, he and the boys set out for the Walters home, and Jackie went to bed, embracing Jason's promise as she slept.

On Saturday morning the boys returned home, and Jason brought over some chocolate chip pancakes, one of his specialties. He was quite the chef, and found cooking a therapeutic exercise.

Sunday was very low-key for the Pattersons. Riley had a soccer game and the family ate at the Sandwich Station for lunch. Archie had the day off.

On Monday after she arrived at Treasures, Jackie logged into the My Chart app on her phone.

The test results were in!

Conclusion: Uneventful core biopsy of the right breast.
Results: Negative
Addendum: Recommend routine annual mammogram in 12 months

Jackie clutched the phone to her chest, and ran over to the Sandwich Station. Once she saw the word *uneventful*, her worries were assuaged.

And she vowed to go on with life, as Archie suggested.

Chapter Eleven

The Autumn Festival brought out scores of Oakviewites into the crisp October air. Jackie manned the Treasures booth on Friday night and Saturday morning, selling autumnal items that Sabrina had ordered online.

There were pumpkins in all forms—stuffed, ceramic, and wood. And kitchen towels reflecting the season, along with autumn-scented candles.

The crowd loved the wreaths above all else. Sabrina had found a wholesaler who sold them at a great price. They were beautifully crafted and reflected fall colors of burnt orange, yellow, and red.

And were sold out by Saturday afternoon.

Jackie, Jason and the boys had an early dinner Saturday night at Walt's Diner and enjoyed the festivities afterward.

Though the Autumn Festival attractions were more for the little ones, Mikey enjoyed hanging out with Cooper and Riley, and even went on the kiddie train with them.

Mikey bobbed for apples as Jackie's boys cheered him on, reveling in his victory as he raised his head above the water, a Granny Smith apple clamped in his teeth.

His prize was a stuffed teddy bear. He knew exactly to whom he would give it. Lately he'd been hanging out with fellow junior Priscilla Blackwood, and he was very close to asking her out on a date.

The bear would be a perfect gift to bring her.

Jackie and Jason greeted many Oakviewites and members of the Chamber of Commerce, who were all out in full force. She knew that she and Jason were fodder for gossip, but she didn't care. She was just happy to be with the Walters guys.

The group left the festival when Cooper complained of a stomach ache after eating a huge cotton candy, and they all walked home under the moon-kissed sky.

Jackie and Jason held hands as they walked, and, to Jackie, it just seemed natural, like their burgeoning love.

Mid-week found Jackie at home for the entire day--quite an anomaly--as Sabrina and one of the part-timers were doing inventory. There had been a lull in business after the busy summer season, and Sabrina had to let go of one of the summer cashiers.

Jackie had hatched a plan. She would visit Jason at approximately 11:30, the time he left for Oakview Gym every day.

And she would ask Jason to make good on his promise during the stolen moments of the day.

After fixing her hair, and donning perfume, leggings, and a soft yellow sweater, Jackie appeared at the Walters house precisely at 11:30 and was met at the door by Jason, who was decked out in sweats.

He stopped short.

"Want to make good on your promise?" asked Jackie, surprising herself at her uncharacteristic flirting.

Jason's eyes grew large as he asked Jackie in, and, grabbing her hand, headed straight upstairs.

They lay on the bed, and Jason began to undress Jackie. He stopped short after unclasping her bra.

"Can I touch your breast where you had the procedure?" he asked, afraid to hurt her.

"Yes, you can," she reassured him, placing his hand on her right breast. Only a small scar remained in the aftermath of the biopsy.

Slowly, Jason removed all of Jackie's clothing, and reveled in her sweet scent, the same vanilla-hued perfume that he took in at the Bennington gym.

147

He kissed her all over, exploring and kissing, exploring and kissing.

Then, it was Jackie's turn.

She only had three pieces of clothing to deal with, which she jettisoned in minutes: sweatshirt, sweatpants, and underwear.

Jackie and Jason lay on his king-sized bed entwined, and he broke the silence with a little common sense.

"Unknown to Mikey, I have a box of condoms in my bedside table," he said. "Should I use one?"

"Yes, thank you. I am not on the pill," confessed Jackie.

She inexplicably began to cry as Jason held her. Heightened emotions overcame her, as she experienced an elevated joy that she never thought she would feel again.

"Are you okay?" asked Jason in the aftermath of their lovemaking as they clung to one another.

"Oh, yes," replied Jackie. "Oh, yes."

At the dinner table that evening, Cooper posed a question to Jackie.

"Mom, are you going to marry Mr. Walters? I saw him give you googly eyes at the Autumn Festival."

Jackie almost choked as she swallowed her water.

"Oh, honey, no. We are just dating. When a person dates, it means that they are getting to know the other person. Mr. Walters and I are getting to know each other," Jackie explained, hoping that she gave the right answer.

"Okay," replied Riley, as he dug into his dinner.

And Jackie was quick to change the subject to asking about her sons' roses and thorns of the day.

Alone in Treasures the next day, Jackie recounted her loving afternoon with Jason in her mind, and she yearned to repeat it very soon.

She had only made love to two men before Jason—her high school sweetheart Brett James and Patrick.

But she knew she had something special with Jason. She had never cried during lovemaking before, and she attributed it to the intensity that she felt.

She knew that Jason felt it as much as she did. Their needs overcame them, and Jackie answered her needs with tears.

And she longed to be alone with him again.

In the afternoon, her sister-in-law, Cassie, dropped by with little Rosalie in tow.

"Cassie! What a wonderful surprise! Look at this little girl! She is growing so fast!" exclaimed Jackie, as she reached for Rosalie.

"Jackie, Rosalie is putting on the pounds and I need some more clothes for her!" said Cassie, zooming over to the toddler clothing section of Treasures.

"Well, we have lots to choose from, including some Halloween costumes," said Jackie, pointing at the display, which Gus had delivered a few weeks back.

"Oh, how darling!" proclaimed Cassie as she picked up a pumpkin costume, which included shoes and a hat. "And you have Rosalie's size!"

After purchasing the costume and three dresses, Cassie was on her way, and Jackie had her baby fill, an unexpected surprise.

Something to keep her mind off wanting Jason.

Every minute of every day.

The next day, Archie came in with his daily present. Today, his offering was something different: a chicken salad sandwich on a croissant, minus the soup.

Jackie was delighted.

"Oh, Archie! What a wonderful new sandwich! I know that it will be a big hit," exclaimed Jackie, who was ready to dig into it, even though it was 9:00 in the morning.

"Girlfriend, I am expanding my horizons!" proclaimed Archie.

His red apron read "Cooking is love made visible."

Indeed, Archie had much love to give.

Jackie's boys were excited to see Halloween on the horizon. She took them to Party City to pick out new costumes, but the pickings were slim, as the holiday was just a few days away.

Riley chose a Batman costume, and Cooper opted for Spiderman.

Jackie made a note to herself to shop in August next year, not October.

On Halloween night, dinner from the Sandwich Station preceded trick-or-treating, which the Pattersons enjoyed with Jason.

A bit too old for the tradition, Mikey stayed home to pass out candy. Jackie left a full bowl at her doorstep, in hopes that the honor system would magically work out.

Once again, Jason grabbed Jackie's hand as they zigzagged among the streets of Oakview, the boys' pillow cases laden with candy.

When Riley started to yawn, Jackie called it a night. Jason helped her boys to bed, and he joined her in her front room, where they enjoyed glasses of chardonnay.

"What a night!" exclaimed Jackie, as she grabbed Jason's hand and lay back on the love seat.

"I think you need to examine the candy," Jason circumspectly mentioned, "in case there is something suspect."

"Would you like to do that with me?" asked Jackie. "Two heads are better than one."

Together, they did a once-over of her sons' pillow cases, eliminating the questionable offerings.

They were surprised to find pennies and pencils in the mix, and laughed at that discovery.

Jason kissed Jackie at 10:00, calling it a night.

She went for an extra-long hug, making a memory until they could be alone again.

Rachel Timmons sat at her computer in her den, making an outline for her eleventh novel, *Pieces of Me*. She had a deal with her publisher; she submitted a novel every three months, and attended book signings as time and place permitted.

Someone once asked her at a book signing in San Francisco if she had any writing quirks, which she thought was a really good question.

Rachel shared that she always had two computers when she wrote: one to pen the novels, and one to look up synonyms on Thesaurus.com.

And she keeps a huge notebook handy, writing bits of information as she goes along, such as a novel's plot points, chapter by chapter.

She likes to write first thing in the morning, and that is why she works afternoons at Dr. Spencer's office.

And there's always a can of Diet Coke by her side.

Rachel perused November's schedule and saw that she had a signing in Los Angeles right before Thanksgiving.

That's about an hour away from Oakview, Rachel reminded herself. An hour away from reconciliation with my precious sister. An hour away from forgiving her and forgiving myself for allowing all of this time to pass without a reunion.

It's time, she thought, not knowing what she would find upon alighting on her hometown.

It's time.

The Chamber of Commerce commenced on November 5ᵗʰ in Pizza Project #2. Harley welcomed his friends, and included in the agenda was a debriefing of the Autumn Festival.

"Well, since it was my first festival, I thought it was just fabulous," offered Archie. "It got me into the fall spirit!"

Brenda echoed Archie's sentiments, saying, "I totally agree, Archie. I think it was a complete success, at least it was for my restaurant."

Other agenda items included the Chamber's Christmas party, which would be held at Primavera in a party room, the watch party for *Christmas in My Hometown* on December 12, and the Christmas Extravaganza, which Harley mapped out for the newcomers.

"The Christmas Extravaganza is held in the gym at Bennington High because of the weather. It is like the Autumn Festival, but there are no rides. Instead, we have a talent show, and there is a beauty pageant that will crown Miss Oakview for the next year," said Harley.

He continued, "There is a gingerbread house contest, and I will be asking members of the Chamber to volunteer to judge it. And the kids can make ornaments and place them on a small tree that we will raffle off. Other raffle gifts include restaurant gift cards, two nights in the Hope Inn, and gas for a month at Speedy Gas."

The Chamber members, who spearhead the Extravaganza, volunteered for jobs for the weekend event, and Harley called an end to the meeting at 8:45.

When they were alone at Jason's house during his lunch hour, tangled between the sheets after lovemaking, Jackie and Jason discussed plans for Thanksgiving, now three weeks away.

"The boys and I go to Patsy and James's house every Thanksgiving," said Jackie. "You and Mikey are welcome to join us. We stay the night there, and there are tons of bedrooms, but we can't sleep together."

"Then we'll have to take advantage of the times that we can," declared Jason as he took Jackie's face in his hands and kissed her.

Lunch would have to wait.

That evening after dinner, Riley announced that there was a bake sale at Easton the next day. Each student was to bring a dozen goodies.

He went to his crowded backpack and produced a wrinkled flyer.

"Guys, we need to plan for things like a bake sale. And this is a huge reminder that we need to clean out the backpacks every day!" Jackie barked, pointing to each of the boys for emphasis.

After the boys were down for the night, and after perusing recipes and fridge contents, she texted Jason:

I have a chocolate-chip emergency!

The boys informed me tonight that there is a bake sale tomorrow, and each kid has to bring a dozen treats.

I have all of the ingredients for chocolate-chip cookies, except for the chips!

Do you have any I can borrow?

He texted back in seconds.

They call me Mr. Chips because, you know, chocolate-chip pancakes are one of my specialties.

I have dark, milk, and semi-sweet chips, and I have regular and mini ones.

What is your pleasure, my lady?

Surprise me!

After reminding Mikey to hit the hay by 10:00, Jason traversed his lawn to the Pattersons' home, armed with miniature milk chocolate chips.

Jackie had put a pot of decaf coffee on, and they got to work.

Sprinkled between batches of cookies were stolen kisses and hugs.

It felt so good to be in Jason's arms again, Jackie thought, even though kisses and hugs alone were on the menu.

After Jason left at midnight, clutching some cookies for Mikey's lunch that day, Jackie just stopped and said a prayer of thanks for the guy next door.

Chapter Twelve

In his restaurateur circles, Archie had heard lots about Cynthia Watkins. Cynthia, not Cindy: a tough-as-nails new food critic with the *Glendale Gazette*.

Lately, Cynthia has been sniffing around Oakview, terrorizing restaurant owners and staffs with her scathing reviews.

She gave Walt's Diner three out of five stars because her hamburger was well done, not medium well.

She docked the Pizza Project #2 one star because there was a piece of sausage in her pepperoni pizza.

Archie learned that Cynthia's MO was to order a bunch of things on the menu, have one bite of each, and never take doggy bags with her.

That's why she kept her trim figure despite eating for a living.

One of Archie's friends, Hugo Jones of Walt's Diner, labeled Cynthia a "demon dynamo" because of her feistiness and her small stature.

Every time a small woman entered the Sandwich Station, Archie braced himself to take on Cynthia Watkins.

It finally happened: She showed up on a busy Saturday, iPad in tow, when Archie was working the check-out counter.

She seemed to have done her research before she stepped up to the counter and knew exactly what she wanted.

"Good afternoon!" Archie welcomed her, certain that this was the demon. "How may I help you?"

She glanced at his green apron, which today had the saying "Let me bake your day."

Cynthia merely huffed.

"I will have the Butterball Bacon Bomb, corn chowder, Roast Beef au Jus Jus, tomato bisque, and Cheesy Grilled Ham and Cheese," said Cynthia.

"What can I get you to drink?" asked Archie.

She scanned the drink section of the menu and frowned.

"You just have soft drinks and water?"

"Yes, ma'am." Archie was getting a bit nervous.

"Well, then, I'll have a bottled water," Cynthia said curtly.

When she took a seat at her table, Cynthia opened her iPad and glanced around the restaurant, taking notes as she took in the scene.

Very family-oriented restaurant with a huge menu. Crowded on a Saturday afternoon. There is a group of soccer players having a celebration in the party room. Train on the ceiling is impressive. Train theme is evident throughout the place.

Archie himself delivered her food to her, as opposed to calling out the order number.

Cynthia was methodical in her tasting: She took one or two small bites, then hit the iPad for her impressions.

Archie tried not to spy on her but couldn't help it. He was looking for some sort of emotion from her, but she showed none.

For about 30 minutes she tasted and wrote, tasted and wrote.

Then she was gone and Archie let out the breath he was metaphorically holding.

He was terrified of reading the *Glendale Gazette*, but his curiosity got the better of him.

Daily, he drove to Glendale to pick up a copy because he didn't subscribe to the paper.

Three days later, there was Cynthia's review:

Hometown Goodness
by
Cynthia Watkins
Glendale Gazette Food Critic

In Oakview there is a charming new sandwich shop that revolves around an interesting train theme.

The casual, neighborly ambience draws huge crowds, especially on the weekends.

There are four train cars that traverse the restaurant and are suspended from the ceiling. The effect is impressive.

More impressive is the food.

The sandwiches are huge and flavorful, and crafted with fresh ingredients.

I understand that there was a contest to name the Butterball Bacon Bomb, which is the bomb, indeed.

The combination of turkey, bacon and brie cheese is a delicious melding of flavors on toasted sourdough bread.

The Roast Beef au Jus Jus has layers of beef and provolone cheese, with a tasty au jus on the side.

The Cheesy Grilled Ham and Cheese was a scrumptious mixture of succulent ham, grilled onions, and sharp cheddar cheese, a tasty combination.

All three sandwiches were plentiful and satisfying.

As for the soups, I chose the corn chowder and the tomato bisque.

Both were hot, hearty and flavorful.

The corn chowder was thick and brimming with sweet corn in a cheesy sauce.

Dotted with bits of tomato, the bisque was a robust soup, perfect for dunking any grilled cheese sandwich. The Sandwich Station has four varieties of grilled cheese.

The choice of drinks was limited. There was water and soft drinks only.

I might suggest adding a wine list.

For example, the roast beef sandwich would pair well with a nice Cabernet Sauvignon. And I'd pair a crisp white wine—perhaps a Chenin Blanc--with the Butterball Bacon Bomb.

All in all, it was a good experience.

I will definitely return to the Sandwich Station, which I give 4.5 stars.

Archie went straight to Treasures with copies of the paper, fuming as he opened the front door.

"Wine list? This isn't the Saffire Room at the Sheraton!" He snarled as a perplexed Jackie stared in amazement.

"Archie, what in the world are you talking about?" she demanded.

He thrust the *Gazette* in her direction.

Quickly, Jackie read the review and laughed.

"Archie, you got 4.5 stars! That is fantastic!!!" she beamed.

"Cynthia rarely gives 4 stars," she reminded him. "This review is very complimentary."

"You know what it would take to get a liquor license? And you bring a whole other can of worms into the mix when you serve alcohol," barked Archie.

"Well, you don't have to worry about that," Jackie said. "Just bask in the 4.5 stars—you deserve it."

"You are right, BFF! I'll bask in the glory. I'm good at that!" boasted Archie with a huge smile.

Patsy and James met Jackie and her boys for brunch on a Sunday morning at Sandy's Dandies.

Unknown to them, Jackie had embarked on a new romance, thanks to town crier Cooper.

"Grandma and Grandpa, did you know that Mom is dating grumpy old Mr. Walters?" he asked as both Patsy and James whipped their heads in the direction of Jackie.

"Well, this is news!" exclaimed Patsy, taking a pancake break to hear the details.

"Now, Cooper," chided Jackie. "Mr. Walters has been very nice to you lately, hasn't he?"

"I guess," said a humbled Cooper.

Jackie glanced at her parents-in-law.

"It's true. Jason and I have gone out a few times, and he and Mikey went to the Autumn Festival with us. And he went trick-or-treating with me and the boys."

"And he makes really great chocolate-chip pancakes!" Riley chimed in.

Jackie chuckled.

"Jason's a really good cook, and one of his specialties is chocolate-chip pancakes," she said. "The boys love them."

When the boys were out of hearing distance as the group walked toward the Castleberrys' car, Patsy put her arm around her daughter-in-law.

"Are you happy, Jackie?" she inquired.

"Oh, yes," said Jackie. "Very happy."

Chapter Thirteen

It seemed as if Maisie had an admirer that wasn't so secret.

Ben Symons, one of Oakview's oldest citizens at age 85, suddenly started showing up at the cleaners on Maisie's workdays.

He always brought her fresh flowers which he grew in his yard, and he was a dapper dresser.

Ben believed in treating women as queens, a practice he used with his wife Sally until her death six months ago from a heart attack.

Now his sights were set on Maisie.

Ben showed up early on a Monday morning and, with a tip of his hat, bellowed a hearty "Good morning, Maisie!"

He passed a bunch of daisies to her; he'd recently learned that they were her favorite flowers.

"Ben, how thoughtful!" exclaimed Maisie as she grabbed a vase in her back kitchen.

"I told you I'm courtin' you, young lady," replied Ben as Maisie blushed.

"How about a proper date this weekend?" he asked. "We could go to brunch or to the movies or maybe go bowling over at Smashing Pins."

Maisie was torn. Robby was her one and only, as she told Jackie. She never considered being with another man. Ever.

"I'll think about it, Ben."

She really didn't know what to do, so she'd put him off for a day or so.

"Okay," he said, with another tip of the hat. "You have a good day now."

Maisie made a faintly waved goodbye with a tug at her heart and confusion clouding her mind.

Jackie and Jason were enjoying a quiet evening at her house while the boys watched a Disney movie in Cooper's room.

"You know what?" he asked, breaking the comfortable silence. "I really enjoy our time together, whether we are out on a date or at one of our homes. I never thought that I would be in another relationship after Elisabeth died, but here I am. It's a wonderful surprise."

"It is, Jason. It really is. I feel the same way," said Jackie. "Patrick's death was such a shock to me and in some ways, I am still healing from it. But I am so lucky to have you in my life."

"I love you, Jackie," he whispered.

"I love you, too," she replied.

Archie was working at the Sandwich Station on his birthday, having donned an apron decorated with balloons and streamers and that read "Birthday Boy!"

He was looking forward to that evening and his date with Roger at Maison Francais.

It was a busy Saturday, but Archie was only working half day.

Just as he was ringing up a family's order, in walked Laney Prescott, editor of the *Oakview Register*.

She was carrying a balloon with a large H on it, and a single red rose.

"Happy birthday, Archie!" Laney chirped, handing over the balloon and rose.

Archie was befuddled. Why would Laney bring him a rose, and what was up with the H?

She was followed by a succession of Chamber of Commerce members, each with letters and roses.

The last three letters were carried by Jackie and her children. They had D, A, and Y, rounding out HAPPY BIRTHDAY.

The exclamation point and final rose were presented by Roger.

The lunch crowd burst into applause and Archie was teary-eyed and so, so touched.

"This is the nicest birthday present I have ever received," he exclaimed, hugging Roger. "Thank you so much."

"I know that, growing up, you didn't have birthday parties and I wanted to make up for that. Here is your party!" Roger waved his hand in the direction of the balloons.

There was something in Roger's grand gesture that cemented a single thought in Archie's mind: He was a man truly in love.

"Mom, that was really fun!" exclaimed Cooper as the Pattersons exited the Sandwich Station. "Uncle Archie was really surprised."

"Was he ever!" Riley declared. "I think that Uncle Roger did a really good job with his presents."

"Speaking of presents, someone has a birthday coming up soon," stated Jackie, looking straight at Cooper.

"In three more weeks! I can't wait!" Cooper beamed. "Mom, I know that you are surprising me about where we are going."

"I have a huge surprise up my sleeve, and you are going to love it," portended Jackie.

She knew that in a million years Cooper would never guess his birthday venue.

And she was really pleased that she'd chosen it for his 8th birthday.

Jackie was working at Treasures one day when Gus brought her three packages.

She realized then that she knew very little about her UPS man, so she started a conversation with him.

"Gus, I say hello and goodbye to you practically every other day, but I know just a little bit about your life," she announced.

"Tell me about your life," Jackie requested.

"Well, I have been married to my husband, Richard, for three years. He is the manager at Glendale Savings and Loan," stated Gus.

He smiled and added, "We are in the process of adopting a baby girl! Her birth mother is due in January. We will call her Madeline; Maddie for short."

Well, I'll be darned, she thought. So much for assumptions.

Maisie had acquiesced to going on a date with Ben that weekend, but her stomach was in knots the whole week.

She felt as if she were betraying Robby; it just didn't seem right.

Just this once, she told herself. Just this once.

Maisie and Ben had fun at Smashing Pins and split a medium pizza at Primavera before he walked her home.

On her porch, Ben was going in for a kiss when Maisie asked him to stop.

"Ben, this isn't going to work for me," she said softly. "There will only be one man in my life and in my heart, and that is Robby. I hope that you understand."

"I do, my dear. I do," he replied.

"But I can be a really good friend," she announced, perking up.

"Then, good night, my good friend," said Ben, lifting her hand to kiss it.

Chapter Fourteen

Jason was asked to be a guest speaker at a conference for the California Accounting Professionals in late November in San Francisco.

Although he made the commitment months ago, he hated leaving Mikey and the Patterson family for the weekend.

They were already feeling like a blended family, he thought. They seamlessly connected in outings and dinners at home.

As the saying goes, the more the merrier. At least that is true for the Patterson/Walters clan.

The night before he left, he cooked a spaghetti dinner for everyone at his house. Over dinner, he went over the weekend rules.

"Mikey, I am letting you stay by yourself because I trust you," he said, looking directly into his son's eyes for emphasis.

He continued, "This weekend, please don't have any visitors, especially any female visitors. You have your car now, so if you go out, please be home by

10:00. And, if you need help, Mrs. Patterson is right next door."

"Got it, Dad," said Mikey, hearing the rules for about the tenth time, but not complaining.

Mikey really was a fine young man.

Jackie kissed Jason at the door when she and the boys left, and she missed him tremendously when he was gone.

She took him to the airport on Friday, and everyone was there when she picked him up on Sunday afternoon.

He brought gifts of sourdough bread and Ghirardelli chocolate, which made Jackie's boys so happy, as they reminisced about their time spent in San Francisco.

For Jackie, Jason brought a snow globe with a cable car inside, a lovely precursor to the holiday season.

It reminded him of the day he kissed her in Treasures, after she shared the charming Oakview glass domes with him.

It was their first kiss, which was as magical as the snow globes.

Jackie can't say she wasn't warned: On Thursday night, a voicemail from Easton Academy's principal announced that school would be closed on Friday because of the flu that was ravaging the campus.

One nurse wasn't enough to handle the throngs of students who came through her door.

By Friday night, the flu hit her children hard. All three Pattersons were up most of the night, and the boys were as sick as dogs, as the saying goes.

Cooper and Riley always got sick mostly in tandem; rarely did one fall ill when the other didn't.

Again, Jackie addressed her ghost: "Patrick! You should be here to help me! It is so hard without you!"

On Saturday, Archie delivered soup and sandwiches, but didn't come inside the house. He was deathly afraid of being sick; his life was just too busy.

By Sunday, the boys were bouncing off the walls, and Jackie was scrambling to clean up the house when Jason called. He was concerned about her after their quick call on Saturday morning.

Again, he asked if he could help.

She decided to go for broke.

"You know what, Jason? I could really use some pampering and some dinner. I have nothing in the refrigerator, as the boys were ravenous today," she declared, sheer exhaustion setting in.

"You've got it!" bellowed Jason. "Draw your bath and I will be right over with leftover vegetable lasagna and garlic bread. And I will bring stuff to make sandwiches for the boys tomorrow."

"You are a godsend!" Jackie exclaimed as Jason came through the door.

The place was a mess with unfolded laundry on the couches and Riley and Cooper running around.

It wasn't called the 24-hour flu for nothing.

Jason took over and pointed Jackie to the bathroom. Then he fed the boys and got to work.

He emptied the dryer, folded the clothes, and put the leftover lasagna in containers for Jackie's lunch tomorrow.

He put fresh sheets on the boys' beds and emptied the kitchen trash.

When Jason brought some food into the bathroom, he saw that Jackie had fallen asleep on her bath pillow.

She looked angelic and completely at peace, a great juxtaposition to the past 48 hours.

He shook her gently, and she awoke with a start.

"Oh, Jason! I can't believe I feel asleep! This water is freezing cold!"

He wrapped her in a towel and hugged her tight, thinking that the future could be so great with her.

Just simply being together would be more than enough for him. For forever.

Archie was working near closing time when a huge group descended on the restaurant. He almost turned them away and was glad he didn't.

Scanning the crowd, he spied none other than Jennifer Lopez in the center of it. In the flesh!

Archie nearly fainted.

JLo looked luminous, her long, flowing hair falling to her waist.

She was wearing jeans and a fur jacket over a white turtleneck.

She was someone Archie greatly admired, coming from his dancing roots.

As a matter of fact, he learned to dance by watching her videos in his bedroom alone.

His Christian parents would have never understood his passion, which brought him to Las Vegas for several years. He had made the rounds dancing in clubs and hotels.

"Miss Lopez! Welcome to the Sandwich Station!" chirped Archie, suddenly getting it together.

"This place is adorable, as are you!" she responded, looking at his apron that read "King of the kitchen," a crown above the saying.

Archie nearly died. JLo thinks I'm adorable!

It seemed that her dancers were accompanying the star, as she had just finished a show at the Oakview Arena. Archie's place was one of only a few restaurants that were still open.

While the entourage enjoyed soup and sandwiches, Archie slipped a JLo CD into his boom box and turned up the volume.

He couldn't help himself and started dancing to "Jenny from the Block."

He knew every part of the routine.

When Jennifer came forward to join him, he handed his phone to one of her dancers.

Without his phone's video, no one would believe this story.

When they were finished dancing, and after Archie nailed the routine, everyone clapped for the duo.

After Archie informed JLo that he learned dancing from watching her, she replied, "You were an excellent student, Archie!"

Again, he nearly fainted.

What a dream come true, he thought.

Jackie and Jason dropped off Cooper and Riley at the Castleberrys for the weekend and checked into the Pelican Inn, just five minutes away and right on the ocean.

James and Patsy were very cordial to Jason, and Jackie breathed a sigh of relief. She felt like a teenager dating for the first time and getting her parents' approval of the boy.

Despite the November cold, Jackie and Jason kept each other warm in their room at the B &B, luxuriating in the whirlpool tub with the fireplace ablaze, followed by dining in the beautiful rustic restaurant.

They took a long walk on the beach on Saturday morning after their room-service breakfast.

Jackie thought that she knew everything about Jason, but learned that he was homecoming king at Mount Olive High School, where he grew up.

He was on the surfing team and math team, and played hockey all through high school.

He met Elisabeth at a Starbucks in Glendale; she was a barista and made the best cappuccinos.

"I thought that the sun rose and set in Elisabeth's eyes," Jason stated poetically. "We were a great match, and we both wanted the same things in life: to marry, have kids, and live a great life."

Jackie squeezed his hand, feeling sympatico.

"We wanted the same," she replied. "It's funny how fate changes everything."

Jackie shared that she met Archie at Bennington High School, and that they were in several plays and musicals together.

"Can you imagine my playing Sandy and Archie portraying Danny from *Grease*?" she asked. "I still know all of the songs by heart, and once in a while, Archie and I just break out in song!"

She connected with Patrick at a party when she was home from the University of Southern California on summer break, and within the year, they were married.

Jackie discussed her estrangement from Rachel, which she had touched on before.

It still hurts, she thought, as much as it did ten years ago.

When they were having lunch in the dining room, the mood had changed from bittersweet to jovial as they shared more stories.

"I have a confession to make," she admitted, looking straight into his eyes.

"I used to have this mantra that I said every time I was mad or frustrated with you."

"A mantra?" Jason asked, looking skeptical. "Okay, let's hear it."

"Cretin. Monster. Jerk!" replied Jackie, looking embarrassed.

Jason guffawed at the thought.

"Well, I deserved that, I suppose," he said. "I was all of those things, and then some.

"What would be your mantra today?" he asked.

"Wonderful. Loving. Giving."

Jackie merely smiled.

Chapter Fifteen

The fall had been a busy season for Jackie and her sons, with soccer and baseball continuing until the end of the year.

She continued to read to her sons' classes, and her friendship with Caroline Williams grew stronger as she visited with her before her reading sessions. They had even made a date for coffee, and Caroline had made a trip to Treasures when her sister had a little girl. The infant clothes were especially darling.

Cooper's 8th birthday party was celebrated in mid-November in the party room of the Glendale Hornets' baseball stadium. The Hornets were a farm team of the Los Angeles Angels.

Though it was the off-season for the team, two of the Hornets came decked out in their uniforms and signed autographs for the partygoers. Cooper was in heaven the whole time.

Jackie had enlisted both Walters men for help at the party, and she was glad to have them along.

Mikey enjoyed the arcade adjacent to the party room with Cooper's classmates, and he took on Riley in a game of foosball which, surprisingly, Riley won.

The Patterson family was looking forward to Thanksgiving, when they could see all of their relatives and enjoy a feast with all of the trimmings.

Jackie had explained to Cooper and Riley that Jason and Mikey would be joining the Patterson clan, and the boys jumped for joy.

"Are they going to spend the night, too?" asked Riley.

"Yes, honey, they are," replied Jackie, who was secretly plotting a way to sneak into Jason's room under the cover of nightfall.

"Well, Mom, do you think that Mr. Walters might make his world-famous chocolate-chip pancakes?" asked Cooper.

Jackie laughed and said, "I don't know. I suppose it won't hurt to ask him."

Yikes! thought Jackie, Jason would be making breakfast for over 30 people! She'd have to volunteer to be Mr. Chips' sous chef.

While she and Sabrina were working on the Monday of the week of Thanksgiving, Archie popped in with some cream of broccoli soup and turkey sandwiches, which he called a "harbinger of Thanksgiving."

Today his orange apron was devoted to the holiday, and read "Hot stuff*ing* coming through!"

"So, girls, I hope you have a wonderful turkey day! I would love to join you but Roger and I are going to have some R & R at Caesar's Palace in Vegas," he shared.

"Craps and buffets and manicures, oh, my!" Archie did a little dance around Treasures, reveling in the thought of enjoying Las Vegas with his beloved Roger.

Just then, the door to Treasures opened up, and a beautiful woman with long brunette curls entered the shop. She had on a gorgeous flowing dress in autumnal colors and had captivating hazel eyes.

She was carrying a box.

Archie stopped dancing, Sabrina's eyebrows raised, and Jackie stared in amazement at Rachel.

Her sister had come home.

The box discarded, Rachel flew into Jackie's arms and the two began to sob. Quietly, Archie and Sabrina fled Treasures and dashed into the Sandwich Station, gabbing as they went along.

"Sabrina! I think that's Jackie's long-lost sister Rachel!" he announced, and she agreed.

"Archie, it has been like ten years since they have seen each other!" she said, taking a seat and grabbing a menu, deciding on an early lunch.

Archie joined her, and over lunch they continued their speculation and both admitted that they couldn't wait to have a long chat with Jackie.

Back at Treasures, Rachel and Jackie continued to hold each other, their sobs rendering them unable to speak.

One shopper opened to front door, then quickly closed it, not wanting to intrude on the emotional moment.

Finally, Rachel was forthcoming and offered an apology.

"Jackie, I am so, so sorry for what I did to you. It was not right for me to leave you and Oakview, but I was very selfish and very self-centered. And I was embarrassed because I thought I was so in love with Patrick, and I knew that love wasn't reciprocated," Rachel said, disengaging from Jackie.

"I just didn't know what to do, so I ran," she winced, revisiting the stinging memories. "I have been living in Redding, in Northern California, since then. I work for an internist part-time and I write romance novels."

Rachel pointed to the parcel. "This box contains all of my published books thus far, all inscribed for you."

She continued, "I am sorry, too, for all of the memories I could have made in the past ten years. But I hope to make new ones with you."

"How did you find me?" inquired Jackie.

"I went straight to the Oakview Police Department, and that really cute Chief of Police pointed me to Main Street Treasures. This is a really darling shop. Are you the owner?"

"Oh, no," said Jackie. "My sister-in-law, Sabrina, owns it. I work part-time since she returned from maternity leave, but I think she might give up working, as she misses her baby girl so much."

"Do you have children?" asked Rachel.

"Yes, I have two boys. Riley is 6, and Cooper is 8. It is just the three of us. Patrick died of a heart attack last year."

"Oh, Jackie! I am so sorry! And I am so sorry that I wasn't here to help you." Rachel went in for another hug.

There was much catching up for the sisters; they had just scratched the surface.

Maisie was just opening up her shop when Ben bounded in, not carrying his customary bouquet.

"Good day, Maisie!" Ben bellowed. "How are you?"

"Just great, Ben! How's it going?" Maisie asked.

"Well, I've come to make an announcement," he stated. "I'm dating Pearl Hopkins who works at Sunny Horizons Convalescent Home. She is one of the administrators and is a really nice lady," he beamed.

"Well, good for you, Ben. Good for you!" replied a sincere Maisie.

Thanksgiving brought another Patterson feast, but this time the numbers had risen to 17 adults and

20 children with the addition of Rachel, Jason, and Mikey, and minus Archie.

Patsy proved to be the hostess with the mostest, as always, her home an autumnal dream.

Rachel took in the wonderful chaotic atmosphere, with children running around, babies being passed from loved one to loved one, and the aroma of comingled Thanksgiving offerings swirling about the house.

It would take her a long time to learn all of the names of the Patterson clan, but she didn't care.

Sharing what they were most thankful for, as is a Patterson tradition on Thanksgiving, Rachel knew what she would say when it came to her turn.

She glanced around the room before she spoke.

"I am thankful to meet all of you. What a lovely family you have! And I am thankful that my sister and her boys are finally in my life. I look forward to getting to know all of you and to reconnecting with my hometown once again."

The clan exploded into spontaneous applause and Rachel grabbed Jackie's hand and said a silent prayer of thanks that she is now the newest member of this wonderful Patterson family.

Epilogue

On December 12, the Oakview community descended upon the gym at Bennington High School, their lawn chairs and blankets covering the gym floor, and ready for their watch party for *Christmas in My Hometown*.

Thankfully, George McAlister, the Bennington Boys' Varsity Basketball coach, planned to have the floor refurbished during Christmas vacation, so the inevitable scratches were no problem.

Representatives from KFUNN and the *Oakview Register* were at the ready to play pre-movie music and to record the moment for tomorrow's paper.

Food trucks abounded in the student parking lot; they were the same ones that the activities director used for dances: the Barbecue Brothers, Funky Taco, Chronic Pizza, and for a bit of dessert, Donut Stop Me Now and Red Velvet Crush, which specialized in cupcakes.

Inside the gym, student entrepreneurs sold treats to bolster their budgets. Song leaders sold popcorn; the MUN team offered soft drinks; candy was supplied by the Academic Decathlon group; and the baseball program sold hot dogs and hamburgers.

The crowd was pumped up and ready for their collective film debut.

Mayor Max introduced Jonathan Price, the executive producer of *Christmas in My Hometown*.

"Thank you, citizens of Oakview, for allowing us to film our movie on your streets and in your homes and businesses. I know that it was an imposition, but you were graceful and generous," Price said.

He handed Max a plaque that was inscribed to the community of Oakview, and offered thanks from the Hallmark Channel. It would hang in the bank from now on.

Max offered a few of his own words.

"Oakviewites, the time has come for you to make your debut as actors in a Hallmark movie! How wonderful for our community! Thank you to Principal Patterson and to Coach McAlister for allowing us to use the biggest building in our city for this watch party. And thank you, citizens of Oakview, for your patience, cooperation, and participation in *Christmas in My Hometown*!" he bellowed.

He continued, "So, let the movie begin! Look closely—you might see yourself!"

With that, the BTV crew started playing the movie on a huge screen, the crowd cheering loudly.

Maisie was set up with Bill, Veronica, and little Olivia close to the screen. She instinctively touched

Veronica's growing bump, happily awaiting the arrival of a baby boy in three months that the Hamiltons would call Robert William after Maisie's husband.

Jackie's posse was big: Archie, Roger, Jason, Mikey, Rachel, Cooper, Riley and, surprisingly, Priscilla Blackwood, whom Mikey personally invited.

Mikey and Priscilla held hands during the movie, marking their first date, even though tons of people were witness to it. They shared a bag of popcorn and sodas, supporting their classmates' endeavors.

Archie was happy to share this moment with Roger, who delighted in seeing his boyfriend in scenes in the movie.

Little did he know, but there would be something special in Roger's stocking at Christmas: an engagement band matching the one that he and Archie would wear in their engagement and for life.

Rachel hadn't disclosed this to Jackie, but she had decided to leave her Redding home and relocate to Oakview. Her primary job would be as a romance novelist; she decided to abandon the idea of working in a doctor's office.

She recently received the wonderful news that her first novel, *All of My Life*, would be picked up by Lifetime and made into a movie. Rachel would be on hand for the filming in Los Angeles, all the more reason to move an hour away.

Jackie was so happy at this moment. She and Jason had established themselves as a couple, and their boys were so happy to interact on family outings.

Jason revealed that he was Jackie's silent benefactor, which made her love him even more.

Little did she know, but she and her BFF would both receive engagement rings at Christmas.

Perhaps a double wedding was in the offing.

Whatever happens, Jackie will be proud to become Mrs. Jacklyn Walters and to marry the guy next door.

Photo by Noelle Reminiskey

About the Author

When Tanya Katnic was reading a romance novel every week, her husband, Andrew, challenged her to write a book of her own. She made a promise to herself that one day she would pen her own novel. Fast forward past her career as a high school English and journalism teacher, and the promise was fulfilled. *Treasures of the Heart* is her third tome, following on the heels of *Our Mother Away From Home* and *A Recipe For Love.*

CPSIA information can be obtained
at www.ICGtesting.com
Printed in the USA
LVHW081614130122
708519LV00016B/1032